Changes & Dreams

for my sons, Patrick and Christopher

Changes & Dreams

Glenda Beagan

Glenda Beagan

seren

seren is the book imprint
of Poetry Wales Press Ltd
First Floor, 2 Wyndham Street,
Bridgend, CF31 1EF
Wales

A British Library Cataloguing in Publication Data record
for this book is available from the CIP Office

ISBN 1-85411-173-6

The publisher acknowledges the financial support of the Arts Council of Wales

Cover design by Debbie Maidment

Printed in Plantin by
Creative Print and Design, Ebbw Vale

Contents

Changes and Dreams

There were these great splayed trees and a barn.

Now, suddenly, as the bus turned unexpectedly up from the drizzling sea road, steeply through February hedges and rags of sky, she caught this glimpse. Just that. And then only for a jolting moment — there on that ridge on the other side, seen between a stand of larches, a solitary farm. But try as she might afterwards, turning in her seat and craning, trees and barn eluded her as the bus dipped and rocked, to climb again at a different angle towards the town.

It was as if she'd imagined them, those totem trees of childhood. Even then they'd been ancient. Huge crack willows, branches lurching, a creaking galleon in high winds. Greengrey blades, with, in one wet summer, a blight on them like scabs, like small gold blisters.

She never came this way. Never came on the slow bus, the stopping bus that took for ever, but this time there was time to kill and she didn't want to wait for the Limited Stop. She'd only have to hang around the shops, then, tempted to spend. So that was why she'd come this way.

A fluke, really. Seeing them.

Birchenholt, she turned the word over quietly in her head. I haven't been back for years.

But she was back now, transported there, like it or not. Wishing, perhaps, that she hadn't looked that way. Tilted back like the old egg-timer on the white-tiled sill in the pantry there. It was all so clear, those jugs of milk standing in water on the larder shelf, replenished cold from the well, fringed scarves of muslin weighted with beads. And the meat safe's fine zinc mesh. Yes, jolted home, though Birchenholt was never home really, it was too special for that. Jolted as sand is, before it runs and heaps again, until time pours it, time and a succession of hands, whose, it hardly matters, in the context of all that ancientness. That going back. Mottled, strong, sinewy, a host of hands. Then, brown eggs in bowls, flung orchards of laundry.

She hears David's voice again, sees the pair of them striding down the sloped lawn from Cae Abbot.

They are eight, maybe nine years old and the world is a wonderful place. It's the summer holidays. They have all the time they need to explore, to invent, to have adventures. Already the gulf between them is there, though, if unrecognised. David is being sent away to school, to prepare him for a very different life from hers. Briefly, though, it seems they are peas in a pod, inseparable.

I loved him even then, she thinks, silly though it sounds. I wonder where he is now?

The trees she'd glimpsed in the distance, high on their ridge, had been transfigured. They'd lost their shape, their sense of splendid command. Regal trees. Gods in their prime. But gods don't change, do they? They stay the same, untouched by time's ravages. Their changelessness is the whole point after all.

Unlike those torn giants, the wind whistling in them and in the twisted corrugated iron. If great trees like that can slice and fall, and barns can totter, so all that's left is the rib-cage, bare bones and rust, where does that leave us, David?

* * * *

And now the sky in the west has thin pink strands in its smokiness. The windows of the bus are steamed up, the air in it warmed and sleepy with breathing. She rubs a patch in the moisture so she can see, just as they pass the old windmill, so odd among those trim redbrick houses, down its track with new cherry trees, set back on its windy edge. It's a house now, a strong shape where in those long ago days there'd been only ruin; a home, splendidly converted, clean white, spruced sails static, small asymmetrical windows glinting. Changes. Was there nowhere she could go without memories of how things used to be, without echoes of before? That old grey stone stump in its tangle of nettles where a whole flock of tiny creamy daytime moths would rise up like animated dust particles, and the air smelled of dank weeds and mattresses and dog muck, was handsome now, was heritage. Somehow she'd liked it best as it used to be, before they renovated it, titivated it.

Heritage ....

And she thought of the Chinese lantern tree at Cae Abbot. Its proper name, its *botanical* name, (and she could hear Cecil's rich wheeziness murmuring his litany of Latinisms, as much gone, as much vanished as the enclosure of peace that was his garden) she'd never known, had never actually needed to discover. It was enough to call it the Chinese lantern tree.

Enough. Satis — which, Cecil would say, he who'd always had more than enough of everything and therefore didn't know any different — means a copious adequacy. And who could possibly want more than that?

She saw the path again, that path of plenty.

Remembering it as a crumbling, loving grey snake, pitted with holes and roots and spurts of weed, plantains, fists of couch grass, the occasional foxglove. Then, it was the summer of love, of 'O' levels and David, the start of it, well no, the different note, and that twinkling disreputable party of *oitinerants*, as Nettie called them, affectionately mimicking Theresa's accent, the girl she'd shared a room with under the eaves of the tall house in Sefton Park where she'd been in service; that belching monster of smoke and bitumen in the lane, smells of burning and diesel, sights of crinkle flame, long devilish rakes like giant toasting forks. Somewhere, beyond them and their world of sweat, their half-shy leering, tattoos and beerguts, charred corduroy breeches, worlds of meadow-sweet had opened through a gate, through tracts of dry earth, cattle ruts, pineapple mayweed.

A wood and an ash tree and you, David. You. And now she would smile at the memory of it, or would have done, if that part of her life was not already overlaid with bitterness. Perhaps, despite herself, she does smile inwardly.

And when you came out of the wood, lavish in your own eased glorying in each other's bodies, and more alive than you'll ever be again, you find that loving path round the house, (dented and worn and footrubbed away into its own reassuring self of leaf and tendril and bright green clump) is now a smooth wet black new strongsmelling river of tar. And nothing can be the same again. Ever.

Especially when you find out how they asked too much for the job, and how Cecil lost his temper, said it was daylight robbery and no, he wouldn't be paying, and how he'd had another of his funny turns, as Nettie called them, and how when your mother and father came back the following day, David, to find an irate Irish gaffer insisting on his money, and learned how Cecil had arranged the tarmacing off his own bat, never thought twice, just went along with it as if he had the right to make decisions, as if he owned the place, for heaven's sake, he collapsed, right there, outside on the still soft and, as it turned out, fatal path.

And died two hours later in hospital. And, who knows, perhaps, the death of Cecil, the black sheep who was somehow so much more lovable than all the white ones put together, marked the beginning of the end at Cae Abbot.

And of us.

* * * *

I am writing this because I want a shape that makes sense. I want my life to have a shape, perhaps even a purpose. To do this I started off by looking at myself from the outside. That helps sometimes. I see things more clearly that way, what David would call objective.

There are four generations of us in this house. There's Tom, the focus of all our attention who'll be having his first birthday next month. Then there's Kerry, his mother, my daughter, and she's seventeen. I'm forty-four and right now I feel like I'm a hundred and fifty. And the house is my mother's house. It's also the house of my childhood, so to come back here is to admit defeat, isn't it? As if all those intervening years count for nothing. And I don't want to think like this.

Last night I was trying to salvage a pair of curtains. I'd decided to do this because I thought it would settle me, take my mind off all the disturbing ideas I'd had ever since catching that glimpse of the trees and the barn at Birchenholt. I got off the bus and felt restless. And angry. I'd had big ideas of my own, once upon a time. That journey, taking me home by such a roundabout route, had opened so many locked doors and windows. I was seeing things with a new intensity, all the colours clear and rich, all the outlines sharp. Now I was sitting at the back of the room, my chair against the wall, with these great swathes of worn material hemming me in. I was concentrating, literally, on the matter in hand, watching the weaving needle as I darned.

My mother, (let's call her Nain shall we, since Kerry does and I always think of her as Nain now), was half doing a crossword, half listening to Newsnight. The room was warm, too warm, but she's always felt the cold and likes to sit right up on top of the blazing logs, practically, with me in the far corner as far away as I can get but still sweltering, and I wasn't paying much attention.

I used to hate t.v. as background. If I watched, I watched properly, none of this wallpaper effect thank you. Anyway here's this interview with Douglas Hurd about Maastricht. Ratification. Protocol. Prerogatives. The Social Chapter. Expert legal advice. Confusion and cynicism. He looks uncomfortable, I'll give him that, and he's being grilled for sure, so when, after a whole tissue of fudge and mudge and waffle, he comes out with those words — Now it is clear, it is clear — I just want to laugh.

The words wash over me. These curtains are for the tiny front bedroom where Kerry sleeps, with Tom in the cot beside her. What sort of world will it be for you Tom, this world you'll grow up in? A world of violence, of waste, of hatred. And a world still full of ordinary people, doing their best, trying to get by. A quieter world, that, which doesn't make the headlines.

Three women, three mothers, and one of these herself not much more than a child, sat together in a hot bright room, in an end of terrace house in a February valley. With its decaying trees and remnants of abandoned industry, it has a sad look and a strange empty smell, but it has beauty too, in its way, especially when spring gets here properly, the blackthorn in blossom, wood anemones, wood sorrel, and in the skittering stream that runs clear now, little clumps of golden saxifrage grow on the banks and on rocky little islands. Rooks are already repairing their nests in the tallest ash trees, and later there'll be the strong smell of wild garlic everywhere. Cars don't often come down here. It's a bit of a dead end really, but that suits us.

Now it is clear, it is clear.

I wish it was. I wish I could look ahead to something more than living on the breadline. At least by looking after Tom, I'm giving Kerry a chance to carry on at college. Perhaps things will work out in the end.

I've done my best with these curtains. Tomorrow I'll walk up to Birchenholt, with Tom in the buggy. Not all the way, though. I'll get the bus as far as Smithy Corner. I wonder what the old place is like now. Does anyone still live there?

I remember how David and I would walk up there on a hot cloudless day. Nettie would give us lemonade, the home-made stuff, and we'd sit in the kitchen, the copper pans hanging on hooks above our heads over the great stone fireplace, catching in their polished circles the tilting bustle of the place, the swags of heavy and musty-scented sage that would start me sneezing, the evergreen limbs of small-leafed rosemary. Then we went out the back, across the orchard and on to the ridge. That's where the magnificent willows had whined and billowed in the high winds. Dominating my memories of our childhood visits is the one we made much later. I remember how we made love on the scratchy ground within that half bright half shadowed world of low, wide branches. That was our first summer as lovers, our last as friends.

That's how it goes.

After Cecil died there was a different atmosphere at Cae Abbot and though we continued to walk between the two so very different places, nothing was the same. There was no room for me anymore in your scheme of things. Let's face it, what did we have in common, apart from the funny friendship we'd built up over twelve or so years? And it was all because Nettie, my aunt, worked two days at Birchenholt and three at Cae Abbot, just occasionally taking me along with her because my own mother, with her great brood of children, was glad to have even one off her hands.

Our lives were about to follow their opposing destinies.

Doesn't that sound grand?

I felt that it wasn't over though, our connection. Even when I married Ray and you'd just graduated from Oxford, I felt our old bond wasn't severed. I went with Ray to live in his flat at the garage and that's where we stayed. He drank more and more heavily. The whole thing collapsed, the business, our home, his health, everything. Gone. You were good looking Ray, in that swarthy, earthy way of yours. So different from fair, sharp featured David. His fastidiousness.

My journey up to Birchenholt tomorrow would be something of a pilgrimage, wouldn't it? Does a memory still haunt the place, of two young lovers, of us?

* * * *

'Make sure you've got him properly wrapped up. It looks sunny and bright but it's still only February.'

'I know, mum,' I say, rather irritated. I'm a middle aged woman, for heaven's sake, quite capable of looking after my own grandchild. Tom's growing so fast and I'm really appreciating this opportunity of being close to every precious milestone. Unlike Kerry before him Tom has a sunny disposition. I've never known a child so easy to please. He's bright as a button but he has a kind of serenity about him too. As we set off into the chill, clear air he's looking about him with interest, crooning a low-noted song of contentment to himself and flicking the red and yellow rings of that toy Kerry's strung along the front of the buggy.

We're only waiting two minutes or so when the bus arrives. I struggle with the buggy, Tom parked awkwardly over my shoulder. We're not in the bus for long before we reach Smithy Corner — funny how the old names survive, the smithy was a memory even when I was a child. There's a whole new housing estate appeared where the fields were, and the little strip of wood, hazels mostly, some coppiced long ago. That's gone though perhaps a remnant of it lingers as a hedge at the end of new back gardens. I leave the houses behind and set off up the steep hill to Birchenholt. It's no joke pushing a buggy up here and I'm just a bit nervous. This is a lonely place. In the old days we children played up hill and down dale with never a qualm. How different it is now.

The road has a little trickle of rainwater running down on the left hand side. There's been frost damage too, the surface being quite eaten into, and this, together with the dark presence of the heavy winter trees that line both sides of the hill we're still steadily climbing, adds to the eerie atmosphere. If I wasn't so determined to get up to Birchenholt again after all these years, just to see what the place is like now, I'd be happy to turn round and wind my way back to light and civilization. The road gets wetter, the trickle is more like a stream, the water constantly glugging and lisping as we climb, then dripping continually somewhere out of sight. Tom has stopped his gentle crooning song. The state of the road makes me think it can't get much traffic. Perhaps the place is abandoned. My legs are aching, the calf muscles strained, and just as I begin to wonder how long this is going to take, we're there. At last.

I'd forgotten just how marvellous the view from Birchenholt is. I'm glad to pause and get my breath, looking down at sea and sea road on the one side, green hills and white farms on the other. You could draw a line with a pencil along the landscape. North east of it, within sight of the Wirral, the older places still have solid Saxon names, like Birchenholt itself, or mongrel names like Cae Abbot. South of this line the farms have only Welsh names, Y Gadlys, Rhiwbwys, Pant yr Hespin. Here we seem to be standing on a frontier. I look towards the farm buildings themselves, now, half anticipating what I see.

It's a sad sight, on the verge of derelict, and boarded up to deter kids and squatters. Poor Birchenholt. I suppose you could describe it as a splendid instance of vernacular architecture, an unusually fine collection of agricultural buildings. It must have been the state of the art in farm buildings of its day, all harmonised warm brick with striking gables. The house itself, a low huddle of red roofs, layered, one behind the other, is pretty much as it used to be. It's such a shame to see it empty, though, when it used to be so alive.

For me it speaks volumes of personal history.

How eager, how hopeful I'd been as a child, and how impressionable. I remember waking up on the first day of the summer holidays, so happy I could scarcely contain myself, thinking of all those sunny weeks of freedom stretching endlessly into the distance. David was so important, the centre of it all. It was such a special privilege to be able to go to Cae Abbot for a start. I remember one girl I particularly disliked at school asking me how on earth I'd had permission to play there. There was a strong sense, and I shared it, with typical juvenile snobbery, that David and the people at Cae Abbot, were set apart. They were different from us, like filmstars.

'My aunty Nettie works there,' I announced with pride, innocent of the fact that this, to any one who knew the score, instantly demoted me. I was the niece of an old retainer, that's all. Admittedly Birchenholt didn't have the glamour of Cae Abbot. It was a farm and Cae Abbot was a *mansion.* I loved both places equally, two worlds that provided sheer unclouded happiness, the kind that is a once in a lifetime thing, that doesn't come again.

Tom was looking about him with real interest and chuckling to himself, glad that we were out of the tunnel of trees we'd had to climb through. I was so conscious of clarity and sky around us everywhere.

It was now, turning round the side of the house, that I saw the car.

* * * *

Are there things you've done, said, that come back to haunt you? I should have just slipped away. There was no one in sight. A sprinkle of celandines grew on the bank just by the car and the sunlight was ample and skiddy with brightness.

'Look Tom,' I said, silly nostalgic fool that I was, thinking of past times and past flowers. 'Let's see if you like butter', and I plucked a celandine, twizzed its thin stalk in my fingers and held it under his chin. I don't think he could make out what I was up to and I never got the chance to find out whether celandines make as good a gold blur reflection as buttercups do. He suddenly started to cry, quite unexpectedly. It was so unlike him. He was looking across to the yard of the farm so I turned to see what he'd seen. A man who was fiddling with the catch of the gate, turned towards us. What he saw was a mother and a crying child. What I saw was David.

* * * *

It's a fortnight now since that meeting. After all these years I was surprised he recognised me.

'Mo?' he said. 'It *is* Maureen Williams, isn't it?'

'Maureen Henry, now,' I said stupidly. Tom had stopped crying and was carefully tearing the flower. 'It's such a shame to see Birchenholt empty,' I burbled, filling the empty space between us with a flurry of pointless words. I felt a deep blush climb my neck to my face. I scarcely dared look at him, but he seemed quite collected and calm.

'I thought I'd give the place a last look over,' he said. His hand on the top rung of the gate was a man's hand. I remembered the uncertainty of the boy's. 'My father died three months ago,' he went on, 'and unlike him, I'm prepared to sell for less than it's worth. It sometimes pays to cut your losses.'

'Yes,' I said, as if I knew what I was talking about, then, just for something to say. 'Cae Abbot's certainly been put on the map.'

'That's right. We won the award for the best country hotel after less than two years in operation. It's got quite a reputation as a conference centre now, too.'

'I saw in the paper that you'd bought The Beeches recently.'

'That's right. Well not me, exactly, that was a consortium purchase. Listen, could I give you a lift somewhere? D'you live on the Coppice estate? I'll be going that way. I like the way those houses look, actually. Quite pleased with it as a development, all in all.'

It suddenly occurred to me just how wealthy he was.

'No, no,' I said, 'I walked up here to get some fresh air and exercise. It'll do me good to walk back.'

Tom flung the last remnant of celandine down on the ground. He started to sing his funny monotonous song again.

'You've got a grand little lad there,' David said. 'My youngest is just four.'

I don't really know what was said next. I stood there and watched as he went to the car and reversed it with some difficulty as there wasn't much room. He waved to us as he drove carefully down the rutted track. I stood listening for a while, hearing the faintest far away toot on a horn. He must then have been approaching the one bend on the steep hill. I followed on a few minutes later.

Now two weeks later how do I feel about it? What is there to feel? Sometimes I imagine a different ending to that coincidental meeting. For a start I discreetly let him know that I'm *not* married. And I certainly tell him in no time at all that Tom is my daughter's child, not mine. I make that quite clear. As for him, he's happily married, or seems to be, but when he's in the area he calls to see me. Twice, three times a year, that's all. But that's fine by me. He takes me out for a meal. We talk over old times.

My fantasy doesn't go any further than that. It stops there.

Glut

It was the sight of all that fruit simply rotting on the trees that did it.

'But you can't just barge in there, Gwen.'

'Don't worry,' she said in her most maternal, reassuring way. It worked with children, certainly. Adults it more often left breathless. 'I'll be diplomatic. Honest.'

Bob looked distinctly uneasy.

'And I'll offer to pay for the fruit. I'm going to play it by ear. You'll see. Anyway, I imagine they'll quite simply be ashamed. People like that don't deserve to have an orchard.'

'You going to drive there?'

'No. I'll walk,' she said. 'It's a lovely evening.'

'Can I come, mummy?' Hannah, hair still damp, was sitting in her nightie in the big window chair.

'Not after your bath, dumpling. Don't be silly. I won't be long and I'll read you a story before you go to bed.'

The twins were round the back tinkering with their bikes. Gwen stepped over an inner tube and a chain, an oil-can and assorted spanners.

Was it, if she were honest with herself, partly curiosity, this mission? The fruit was, well, not an excuse, exactly, but she'd never seen the other side of those high grey walls at Llwyn, and the chance of doing so certainly appealed. Those new people had been there nearly a year now. Gwen had kept telling herself they were *bound* to get started on harvesting that bumper crop sooner or later. Well, they hadn't, had they? Already those plums were past their best.

It had been such a hot summer but lately a heavy feeling, a general drab dustiness seemed to hint at its end, spreading a grey haze over everything. The sky was strangely white, opaque. The world felt tired and sticky and over-ripe.

As she stepped through the elaborate, if rusty gates at Llwyn she found the house was just as she'd expected it to be, serene creamy Regency at the end of its curving drive. In front of it stood a huge cedar. On this side the orchard wall was of red brick with what looked like japonica trained along it, and shiny-leaved camellias. Gwen rang the bell, heard it echo an off-key note far away, and seemed to wait ages. A Siamese cat joined her on the step and made its own atonal music.

'You're a very beautiful cat,' Gwen murmured, struck by its lithe good breeding. It was at this moment the door opened, taking her off-guard. She stood face to face with a young woman who, for a moment she thought was just a child, so smallboned, so delicate.

Gwen had no more idea of how to be diplomatic than Atilla the Hun. She came straight to the point.

'As I've been passing recently I couldn't help noticing your plum trees nearest the road. If you're not actually going to pick the plums yourselves I wonder if we could come to an arrangement of some kind ....'

'Oh,' gulped the young woman with what appeared to be relief. 'Yes, of course. You can take as much as you like. I haven't been well enough myself, to pick them, I mean, and my brother won't be back for another two weeks at least. He's in the Aegean. He's a writer, you see.'

'Really? How interesting.' Gwen had heard in the village that these were a bohemian lot.

'Yes, and I'm looking after the cats, and well, convalescing. I've had a post-viral thing. I'm better now than I was, but I get so exhausted. By all means, do help yourself to the fruit. Any time. There are ladders at the back in the old stables. I'll show you now, if you like.'

'Oh no, dear, not now.' What a nervous little creature she was. It was almost as if she was scared of something. And yuppie flu! I ask you! 'I'll pay for the fruit of course.'

'You mustn't think of it. No, I insist. It would be such a shame if it all went to waste, wouldn't it?'

'That's really very kind of you,' said Gwen. She'd been right. The girl *was* ashamed, even if she did have some sort of excuse. But Gwen had to be fair. These were their trees, after all. 'You must at least have some jam and some bottled plums, later. Would it be all right if we came tomorrow?'

'We?'

'I mean my sons. They're twins. They'll be ten on Boxing Day and they're very well behaved. I'll be able to get the fruit picked in half the time with their help. My husband's home tomorrow so he can look after Hannah. She's three. I'm sure you've passed our house many times. It's the old toll-booth cottage. D'you know it?'

'Oh yes. Of course. You've got those big gardens, haven't you. All that soft fruit.'

'That's right. I've had such a busy time getting all the raspberries and blackcurrants frozen. And then there were the peas and the beans ....'

The young woman's eyes seemed to glaze over at this point, but Gwen still had a lot to tell her. She did so much want to keep bees, she said, but Bob wasn't too keen. She still hoped to change his mind about the hens, though. Imagine it, free range eggs for breakfast!

* * * *

The boys were quite smitten by the Plum Lady, as they called her, and the house too. The walled gardens fascinated them, the wonderful light and that rich smell in the orchard, the soft hush underfoot, even if there were too many wasps for comfort. And then there were the stable blocks, all mysterious and cobwebby. They could have stayed there for ever.

Gwen caught only a glimpse of the house's interior, but that glimpse missed nothing. It was strangely bare of furniture, and painted white throughout. Emptiness was the impression she had, cool brilliant emptiness, as the Plum Lady (even Gwen found herself calling her that) led them through to the rear where those rickety ladders were waiting. In the one room she'd seen properly, there was a huge black marble fireplace and very little else, just white rugs and stark primitive looking wall-hangings, a state-of-the-art music centre and an exercise bicycle.

She found herself wondering what this writer brother was like, and had she been less the busy, practical type instead of that type's epitome, she might well have found herself fantasizing about him.

* * * *

Gwen had snatched herself a rare moment of quiet in the back garden among her recipe books. She wanted to see what she could find in the way of wholesome winter stews. She liked to look ahead. She liked to plan. That way she was never caught on the hop.

It was still very hot. Surely there must be a storm soon? Last night there had been rumblings of thunder, but nothing materialised and the boys, normally so easy going, were quarrelsome and awkward. Bob and Hannah (and neither of them could ever be described as easy going) had been particularly difficult, Hannah constantly whining about something or other, Bob moody, ominously silent.

From her deckchair Gwen was watching a late, freak plague of red spider mites milling about on the flagstones. They were dancing vividly on the broad stone window-ledges too. She shivered. They looked so *predatory*.

Then she heard the boys' shouts nearby as they came skidding in round the back on their bikes.

'MUUUURM,' yelled Rhodri. 'MUUUURM, where are you?'

'Here,' Gwen owned up from the bottom of the garden. For once she'd actually been relishing a bit of peace, a bit of time to herself. There was no need to think about tea yet because Bob was going to be late home from work, and Hannah had finally been persuaded to have a rare afternoon nap, but no, she'd spoken too soon, could hear her now, shouting from inside the house, woken by the boys' yells.

'Mum,' Dafydd was almost bursting with excitement. 'Mum, me and Rhodri have just seen an incredible thing.'

'Really?'

'Yes. It's weird, brilliant. You've just got to come and see it. It's a bird. It's an eagle or something. And it's not moving at all.'

'You mean it's dead?'

'No, it's kind of hanging there. It's quite still and it's hanging in the sky. We've been watching it for ages. Its wings are spread out like this, and it looks dead mysterious, mum. Honest.'

Gwen didn't want to pour cold water on their enthusiasm. She always made a point of encouraging all their interests, but right now she was tired. Really tired.

'Come and see, mum. Please,' said Rhodri.

'Where exactly is it?'

'It's sort of on top of the hill behind the market gardens but we can't get very near because there's these geese.'

'Geese?'

'Yes. And when we tried to get across the field they made all this noise and started to chase us.'

'And what am I supposed to do about that, eh? Scare them off? They can be really fierce, geese can. The Romans used them instead of guard dogs, you know. They'd make this awful noise, and then the Romans would know there were strangers about.'

'Just come and see. Go on, mum,' said Rhodri.

'Well, I'm not walking there. Not in this heat. Is there somewhere nearby I can park the car? I'll have to check I've got petrol. Go and get Hannah, for me, will you, one of you?'

'Great, mum,' they chorused.

And Gwen was able to bask in virtue, just a little, which wasn't much compensation really for traipsing up a hillside today, of all days. She just wasn't up to it.

* * * *

Arcs of swerving water with rainbows in them were playing on rows and rows of what would be new potatoes, and the greenhouses were blazing oblongs of white glare.

'Now where can I park?' Gwen groaned.

'That car wasn't there before,' said Dafydd. 'Can you manage to get in behind it?'

'I've got to make sure those people can get out, haven't I?'

That little red car looked strangely familiar. 'You'd think if they're at the market gardens they'd park there, wouldn't you?'

'Perhaps they've come to see the bird, too,' said Rhodri.

'Where can we see it from?' she asked, looking up blankly. Hannah's siesta had done her good. She was stomping vigorously ahead down the lane.

'You can't see it at all till you get round the back of the gardens,' said Dafydd. Or was it Rhodri? Sometimes even Gwen found it hard to tell them apart.

Soon they'd climbed over the stile and were panting up the hillside, and sure enough there was the strange static bird above them, hanging there, just as they'd said. Difficult to tell what it was in silhouette, like this, but Gwen was intrigued.

'Well, I'm not going to brave those geese,' she said, hearing them in the distance. They were out of sight behind a cottage with lots of washing on the line, and yes, how marvellous, gleaming bee hives all in a row by a tall hedge of flowering privet. 'We'll have to find another way round.'

Which they did, after a bit of a detour and a scramble over a wall, a work of art in its way, dry stone at the base then turf on the top, with clumps of moss and fern and a couple of foxgloves.

'I wouldn't normally climb over a wall like this, but we're being very careful not to damage it, aren't we?' Rhodri got across first, and then she lifted Hannah over from her side. 'There you go,' said Gwen heartily.

And there was the bird. It was a bit of a con really. It wasn't an eagle, or anything remotely resembling one. It was a carrion crow suspended on a wire that had been quite invisible from further down. That deceptive half golden appearance was the result of exposure to prolonged strong sunlight, nothing more, its original black bleached to a faded tawny. It was bone dry. Tentatively Gwen touched its stiff feathers as the wire strummed a dull note, pulled taut as it was between a mountain ash and an elder.

The boys were disappointed. 'It's meant to frighten other crows away, I suppose, so they don't try to get at the lambs,' she told them. Not that there were any lambs about now. 'Like they used to put highwaymen up on gibbets in the olden days, so people would know what to expect ....' She was talking to herself. The boys had gone, running off along a track that was probably a bit of that old drovers' road she'd read about, Hannah bellowing after them, 'Wait for me'.

Gwen sat quietly on the trunk of a twisted hawthorn. There was a good view from here, despite the haze, down to the crossroads where their house was, and over there, far away on the other side of the village, was Llwyn. From this angle you got an oblique, almost aerial view of all the outbuildings and that ornate cupola on the old coach-house. Gwen thought of the Plum Lady, her high little-girl-lost voice, her pale tiny hands. She was like a little doll, so fluffy, so helpless, not like an adult at all.

It was just at this moment, as a tearful Hannah reappeared, complaining that the boys had gone off without her and she couldn't catch them up, and would mummy find them and tell them off, that Gwen saw a courting couple emerge from behind some hawthorn clumps higher up the hill. They were hand in hand, quite casual. And then, (and since she'd only seen them out of the corner of her eye, they could, even now, at a pinch, perhaps, have got away with it) they froze. Literally froze. And that's what made her look again. And see. Really see. And realise.

She didn't know what to do. She didn't know where to put herself. They emerged to face her now, they had to, dropping hands as if they'd had nothing to do with each other, yet looking straight towards her, trying to blank their faces into safe neutrality. And Gwen remembered where she'd seen that car, of course she did. It had been parked in front of the house at Llwyn, on the gravel by the shadowing cedar. And she remembered how awkward Bob had looked when he said she was going to go there in the first place, and how relieved, apparently, the Plum Lady had been when she asked if she could have the fruit. It suddenly all made terrible sense.

'Daddy, daddy,' said Hannah, running up to him, pulling at his hand. 'Come and see the funny bird. We came to see the bird.'

Her legs felt as if they didn't belong to her but somehow Gwen made them walk her down the track. She had to get away from them. Now she simply stood there, shouting into hot, still air, while far below the bright arcs of the sprinklers turned, synchronised, and swivelled their diamond water a different way. 'Dafydd,' she shouted, 'Rhodri,' louder and louder into the silence, 'Come on. We're going home now.' As if by calling out the names of her sons, calling them again and again, she could unwork the truth behind her, unwork it all, and, somehow, restore, retrieve, but how, her world.

In the South Country

He heard the Russian woman calling her cats. Every night, before the last of the light, before the fullness of that scented darkness fell on them, the huddled roofs, the heatbaked stone of the houses, 'Minou, Minou,' she would call, again and again. No one knew how many cats there were, or where she came from. She was old, but how old? She was an exile, a mystery.

There were stories, of course. Puzzles and adventures attached themselves to that quizzical face hiding under those large brimmed hats, those scarves. She wore too much rouge. She muttered in her foreign tongue. She kept to herself, accruing legendary significance through silence, through that absence of information she ambled in. It was the luminosity of the hinted exotic, the troubling danger no one can detail.

He had been ill. The pain had gone now, the sheer grappling power of it, but he sensed it was ready again to pounce. He lay on the now quiet bed in the small room with the sloping ceiling. He did not eat for two days, but Jeanne brought him fruit juice. No, he told her, she must not get the doctor. He would be fine, she would see. So he lay there, gritting his teeth, clenching his palms. His face was a clammy grey, the sweat on it constant, in beads, in rivulets.

He loved Le Thoronnet. She had driven him down through countless sun drowsed miles, through vineyards, through fields of blue wide lavender. The sunflowers, acres of them, were, well, there were no words for them .... It was all wonderful. He wished he could tell them back home, but how could he? A kept woman, that might be commonplace enough (even where he came from) but a kept man? It was scandalous, wasn't it?

So? He didn't care. This was the life.

And Jeanne was the woman to share this life with. She was handsome, not pretty, not beautiful, but strong and well-made. She had straight blonde hair, rough to the touch, a little, and very thick. She was sure of herself, of her being, of her body, its muscular compactness, its surprisingly (in the context of all that firmness) pendulous breasts. He knew how to appreciate her. How to treat her. What to say. Not much, but the right words. And money was no problem. She was generous, casual. Anything he wanted was his. He was not curious. He did not ask where it came from.

On the evening of their arrival they had walked up to the abbey among pines. He would remember the dustiness, the scent of resin, the courtyard where a fountain played, the bell that rang out dreamily across the forested hills. They had walked in cool cloisters, and then, back home, in that small, unprepossessing house on the shadowed side of the square, they had unpacked, or rather Jeanne had, since he owned little more than the clothes he stood up in, and then they had made love in that quiet room with a light dry wind whispering under the tiles above their heads, and he knew she owned him and was glad, not knowing how long it would last. Perhaps only for the summer. He would make the best of it.

He went out to breathe the air. Even that was different. It had a different feel. There were plane trees on this side, and opposite, a mulberry. He tugged at a leaf, crumpled it between his fingers, smelt the shards, and then looked up, sensing that someone was watching. She'd appeared from nowhere, the Russian woman. She was looking at him in a knowing way, half leering. How long had she stood there, staring? It was as if she'd got him sussed, as if she saw him as only one in a long line. Did Jeanne always find herself a young man to amuse her in the summer? The Russian woman called her cats in that odd monotone of hers, and two came running, tails aloft, paws raised in delicate welcome. She scooped them up, one under each arm, and left the square still calling, 'Minou, Minou'.

Were they all called Minou? 'Take no notice of her,' Jeanne had said. 'She's half crazy.'

He liked life in the village, at least at the start. The pace was slow. People knew what they wanted and for the most part they had it. It was so different from the city, though working in the bar had been fun in its way, had not asked much of him. These people had a contentment that was somehow infectious. He liked the way the old women would take their chairs outside and chat together as the shadows lengthened. Their French was quite unlike the French he knew, and there was little enough of that, but they seemed to accept him. As the weeks passed, though, he felt they were waiting for something, that he might even be the subject of a wager.

He had not known there were wild boar in the forest. It was a mediaeval notion to him, a fascination. He thought he would like to go with the hunting party, imagined the mystery among the trees, those loping dogs, so elegant, so foreign, the dappled light, asked Jeanne about it, but she had only smiled. And when he'd seen the men of the village assemble, guns on their shoulders, dogs obedient, alert, at their heels, he knew he was alien to them. They wore light jackets, but heavy-shouldered, with leather patches on the elbows. They looked at him coldly, then spoke softly amongst themselves. He was a joke to them, that's all.

So he was restless, was beginning to feel threatened, subtly.

Jeanne took him to meet Bernard, her artist friend in his cool white house outside the village, near the vineyard. He made them ratatouille, slicing courgettes deftly into a bowl. He wore a white shirt of a very fine material, a light voile, and thin trousers of cream linen. Bernard and Jeanne were able to laugh together, warmly, comfortably. They went back a long time these two, he felt, increasingly the outsider, the one apart. He knew he was dispensable. Not liking it, he studied the interior of the house, the canvases, mostly portraits. On the broad sill there were three shedding sunflowers in a blue glaze vase, full bellied like an amphora, and jam jars with sable brushes, variously sized. A curtain hanging on brass rings separated the living area from the studio. Without asking, he slipped through, finding himself face to face with a painting of the Russian woman. It startled him, it was so true. Bernard had captured her jaunty sadness, her toughness, her satire. There was the absurd hat, the filmy scarf about the bony neck, the blobs of rouge like a clown's mask, but there, too, was that expression he'd met himself, a worldly and astute appraisal, a feasting of the intelligence.

'You like it?' Bernard asked.

'Yes. It's very fine.'

'Then you must have it when you go.'

So it was assumed he would be going. Soon, maybe? If so, he must retain some pride. Would leave before Jeanne asked him to, before she was obviously tired of him. He would read the signs.

But then came the pain. The days in bed. The sweating and the fear. And Jeanne had nursed him as if she really cared, maternally, somehow, yet with a sense of distance. Still, he was determined to go soon.

One evening, not long after his illness, he'd heard the cries of 'Minou, Minou' as usual in the quiet stillness outside, and then something else, something terrible, a noise that tore the air and had the inhabitants all rushing out into the street to see what it was. One of the hunting dogs had taken a fancy to a pretty little poodle bitch, the pet of a now weeping child, and they were locked together coitally, grotesque in inappropriate coupling, the little raped one's cries of pain and terror merging with the hound's yelped anger, its disbelief. They were stuck, the one in the other. Jeanne whisked the child away into the house, gave her bread with a dab of apricot, anything, a citrus drink, but all the time those wails, those screams of the beasts outside, were lacerations. There was no distraction. Someone brought a bucket of water, flung it over the locked pair, but to no avail. Then more buckets.

'That poodle will be dead,' someone said, behind him, just as, clutching his side, he reeled and fell with that same agony of days before. But worse this time.

It had been touch and go. Peritonitis. Bernard had rushed him down to the hospital, a zig-zag, headlong rush of a journey, and many miles. After the operation, how long had he been there, a patient? He didn't know. Nor, till later, did he know that Jeanne had paid his bills. She did not come to see him. He knew it was over. That this was it.

Still shaky on his legs, but better, stronger, he left the hospital with an envelope from Jeanne. There was plenty of cash to get him back to England, (but was that where he wanted to be?) and some to spare. On leaving, the nurse in charge of the ward handed him something else, a large flat package, quite heavy, wrapped in brown paper.

No he would not open it. He knew what it was.

Green Eggs and Larches

God was watching.

It seemed to the child, travelling in the slumbery warmth of the bus down lanes deep with rabbits and herb robert, that up there was a place God would choose to live in.

There were the larches. Their shapes were miracles, wind-whittled, they cowered and hunched but were strong too, like old warriors. Or wizards, perhaps.

There was something plain and fierce about those shapes, the spirits of high places. And from up there you had the sense of being able to feel free and apart, the way God must feel she supposed. Looking down was a good feeling. All the sandbanks in the estuary, the treacherous quicks and whirlpools looked small and tame, the water around them milky, or palest green like an opal. It was a trick of distance and light.

'Are we nearly there now?' she kept asking.

Perhaps the journey was the best bit. She wasn't sure she really liked Aunty Ellie. She was a tall big-boned woman, and not at all smiling, even when you first got there and were stood waiting for her to come to the door, in the porch with the tiles of lilies on the walls and the scraper for boots and shoes. It was shaped like a dolphin but with spikes.

Ellie's clothes smelled of mothballs (camphor, mam said it was) and her breath smelt of peppermints. She had furrowed elbows, the lines on them just like tramlines. Her arms were strong-looking, very muscular, because she has to do a man's work, mam told her, and her hands were broad and strong. But it was her face that was frightening, a bit. She had a very staring look even if she wasn't staring. It was the sort of face that knew everything. The child felt that there was nothing you could hide from her. It was as if she already knew all there was to know about you and was disappointed.

So why did she like to go?

Well, there was the journey for a start. And it was somewhere special and different, quite unlike home, their house in Pretoria Terrace with only a thin strip at the back for a garden. Up at Ellie's there was so much space and sky.

They had to change buses to get there and there was half an hour to wait in between. To pass the time they went to the milk-bar on the corner opposite the bus station. Mam would have coffee and she would have a milkshake, lime or raspberry and very frothy, and they would sit in the window if they could.

There was a pub on the other corner, The Volunteer, a disreputable place mam said, with pillars and a kind of verandah outside where the Teddy Boys stood. They all had sleeked black hair and they were all tall and thin and looked like turkeys, the way they strutted about that is, not their shapes.

She had seen turkeys up at Ellie's, being fattened up for Christmas. Most had been ordinary black, with just those bits of red for their combs and wattles. But there was also a pair of what Ellie called her beauties, and they could have been birds of paradise. They were white and gold and red, very noisy and proud. But for all their twirling they'd go the same way as the rest, Ellie'd said with a glint about her.

While mam and Ellie were catching up with their news in the parlour with the harmonium and the pictures of Roman ladies in long white dresses, she went exploring up the still steep hill as far as the larches where God lived.

It was a game she played, imagining places for God to live in, high places they were of course, always. Last time, though, she was restless a bit, and the wind too cold to hang about in. 'Sometimes,' Ellie said, 'the tail end of March is the coldest there is.' It was the east wind that came biting and hissing in the browned old needles of the larch trees, but there were new leaves now, like tiny shaving brushes, the brightest green of all, and anyway, she had a message. She was to go to Y Gadlys and ask for green eggs.

Green eggs. She thought it was a joke, but no, her mother's eyes had told her it was true, so clutching the halfcrowns and wrapped up well, though today the wind was warm with a kind of singing in it, she set off, but this time not as far up as the larches. She was to take the track on the right by the stand for the milk churns. The farm called Y Gadlys wasn't far down.

'Would you like to go and look for some yourself?' asked Mrs Ben Davies. 'The hens like to lay in funny places, sometimes. Look, I've got half a dozen here that Ellie can have, but she wants more than that so your mother can take some back, doesn't she? My little black hens are special. There's not many places you can get green eggs.'

On the table in a large brown bowl there were six green eggs, true enough. Of course they weren't that bright green of the new growing leaves of the larches. But greenish, certainly in a pale way, and not the colour of any eggs she'd ever seen before.

And anyway it would be good to explore up there in the barns at Y Gadlys.

She was good at exploring people said, noticing everything, taking it all in, and able to tell you afterwards exactly what she'd seen. Soon she'd found kittens, tortoiseshell they were, and so pretty with the palest blue eyes, playing among the mallow leaves and in and out of the frame of an old mangle. There were bantam cocks there, too, like splashes of fireworks, their colours so bright.

It was up in the hay loft she'd found the hiding places of the little black hens, where they laid their eggs as secrets, and one was warm still. She had a basket to collect them in, a square basket lined with crumpled sheets of the *Flintshire Herald*, and as she was coming down from the loft, backwards, and carefully, on the ladder, Idwal appeared and held the ladder firm for her. She'd seen him before at Ellie's once, when they were hay-making. She didn't think she liked him much but he must be kind because he had a green egg for her and put it in the bowl. There was a bit of dirty straw still sticking to it.

'I know where they lay,' he'd said. 'There isn't a place where I can't find them.' And after the dark there in the barn, the feathery feel of cobwebs and the heavy smell of grain, it was a surprise to come out blinking into the sunlight.

After that whenever they went to see Ellie she would go on a message for green eggs. And Idwal would always turn up and put an egg in the bowl.

It was summer now and she was nearly nine, and a big girl everyone said. On this hot day, holiday traffic had held up the bus and made them late, but it didn't matter once they got to where Ellie lived, though of course there was that great walk up the hill first. Up at the top there was a wind blowing like a fragrance and it was cool, though still sunny and the whole hill skiddery with the shadows of clouds. Instead of tea this time there was home-made lemonade to drink and tiny strawberries. Little green tomatoes had been put along the hot kitchen window sill all in a row to ripen. Up at Y Gadlys, though, sheltered as it was in the high elbow of the hill, the air was more still, with a clamminess.

This time Idwal had a secret for her, he told her. And not just the extra egg or two he'd always found. She had got used to him by now.

'Come and sit by here with me,' he said. So she went and sat by him in the hay and he put his big hand under her dress.

'You hold by there,' he said. And she did. And afterwards he had an another green egg for her.

Each time she went on the bus to Ellie's there was always the message to Y Gadlys for the green eggs and Idwal would always be there. He would always ask her to sit in the hay with him so she would. She wasn't sure she really liked what he did but he was kind, he must be, finding eggs for her always, and anyway he'd said it was their secret. Could she keep secrets? Solemnly she would nod her head. And he'd always been there, hadn't he? Like the larches, he was part of the place, part of the things that happened there.

She knew he looked forward to her visits. She was special, he told her, and so was he, yes, just like the journey on the bus and the milkshake, the teddy boys on the verandah at The Volunteer, and the bantam cocks and the little black hens. And in spring the lambs in the fields. And sometimes if one of the ewes had died, Ellie would have to rear a pet lamb on the bottle. How she loved to feed it, sitting on the tiled floor among newspapers and old sacking, the feel of its springy gentle wool, so soft, and sometimes it would pee warm and wet down her leg.

Because of being held up in the traffic jam for so long, and you could see it like a many coloured snake writhing along the road down there, like it was miles and miles below them, Idwal had seemed bad tempered when she arrived at last at Y Gadlys. When she went into the barn to look for eggs, he hadn't waited until she found them, appearing afterwards, as if it was part of a pattern, a right order of doing things. No, he'd been cross, a bit, and a bit rough too, though not hurting her. This time, though, he wanted her to do something different, and because he seemed to want it a lot, she got a bit frightened. He was not so friendly at all, this time, but she did what he asked. And then he went funny and juddery and made noises. And she'd not found any eggs yet.

He did not speak to her afterwards. He covered his face with his hands and his arm then, and wanted to hide himself, all of him, it looked like, in the hay.

She did not go back to the house, to Mrs Ben Davies. She slipped past the kitchen window quickly so they wouldn't see. When she got back to Ellie's she said there were no eggs today, but afterwards they must've found the basket on the floor of the barn, just by the ladder where she'd left it.

A few days later, at home after school, her mother came up the garden with a policeman. She was sitting on the swing Dad had rigged up for her in the door of the shed. And she knew it was something to do with Idwal, just like she knew, even then, that she would say nothing at all.

Later, not long later, a week or two maybe, she found out about an incident. That was the word. Yes. Incident. With a girl. But who could that be, if she'd been special, like Idwal said? Anyway, there'd been complaints. And now the policeman was looking at her very hard, asking her if Idwal had ever said anything to her, or touched her, or asked her to do anything she didn't want to do. She kept saying no to everything. He went away in the end.

She didn't go to Ellie's on the bus with her mother anymore. She didn't want to, she said, though she knew she'd miss the different feel of the place, and the journey, and the larches where God lived. Sometimes she wished she could change her mind and go after all. But then she remembered Ellie's staring. And she could see Mrs Ben Davies going into the washhouse for the basket, the smell of the moist air there, starch and soap and boiled cloths. And she knew she couldn't go back, ever.

And she'd catch her mother giving her the same sideways look she'd seen on the policeman's face that time. A look of wanting to ask more, but not knowing how, a look of not believing.

The Man from Kurdistan

'Oh, but I couldn't do that,' she said. 'No, really. I just couldn't.'

And briefly, searingly, I'd seen the dangers of fiction. Not for the first time, but freshly, somehow. Again I remembered all those old fears about writing.

Her frank and very blue German eyes made me squirm a little.

There were seven of us. All women. The youngest in her late thirties, the oldest pushing eighty, maybe. We sat round two tables pushed together in a cream painted room that had once been a chapel schoolroom. A cheese plant soared in the corner, a brief and early tribute to unlikely sophistication. A handwritten notice on the wall told us in Welsh and English that we were forbidden to imbibe intoxicating liquors on the premises. Beyond this, the table and the basic stacking chairs, the room was bare.

The building was the undoubted centre of life in this big scattered village but as we sat there, pens in hands, papers blank before us I wished fervently that we were not next door to a huge discount food store. The warehouses were massive. All day long lorries would come and go. As they reversed out of the large yard they would *beep beep beep beep* constantly. Sometimes it sounded like an orchestra of lorries was tuning up for a big performance. It was not conducive to encouraging our creative efforts at all.

But Helga had been busy.

At the last meeting she'd handed me a thick exercise book chock full of her meticulous handwriting. It was a thoroughly worthy effort, especially bearing in mind that she was not writing in her first language. It gave an account of her life and was for the most part competently written but somewhat dull. Sadly she'd skimped on recording her childhood because here there were nuggets of brightness.

In the years immediately following the war the young Helga had gone to stay with relatives in the country. The writing suddenly took wings. There'd been an old house, a castle almost, with cellars and corridors and strangely shaped turret rooms. There'd been a dried moat full of coppery beech leaves where the children played and hid.

'This is marvellous,' I said. 'It's special and it's different. Can't you give us some more of this?'

'But that is all there was,' said Helga.

'Fictionalise, then,' I said. 'Invent some episodes. Enlarge on this material. Tell us a story, Helga.'

And then came that prompt disavowal. I felt rebuked, as though I were out to corrupt her, steer her away from the clear if commonplace truth into the dubious realm of make-believe. To enlarge, to elaborate, to conjure up new elements would be wrong in her eyes. This was Helga's experience. It was true. It would remain inviolate.

'*No, really. I just couldn't*,' she said.

* * * *

I'd noticed him on the station at Crewe.

There we were on platform eleven in the milling winter crowd and there he was laden with khaki backpacks and bedrolls. It was the earring I saw. It was elaborate, like a small version of those hanging lamps you find in churches sometimes. Or a censer, maybe. It was filigree silver. And it certainly took my eye.

I didn't stare though.

Later, (the train was leaving Chester by now so where had the earring man been in between?) the harassed looking girl with the refreshments trolley asked whether madam would mind if this gentlemen sat beside her.

Well yes, madam did mind. Quite a bit. Territorial imperatives and all that. There were other empty seats further up the carriage, too, so why pick on me? Helpfully though (I was nicely brought up) I moved my big blue holdall and my handbag to make room for him. She wanted to get on with pushing her trolley up the aisle and she needed him out of the way.

I was soon to see why. He was drunk. Very.

As he eased himself into the seat next to me I was met by a waft of spirits. It was so sharp, so strong. It wasn't so much that he was smelling of drink in the ordinary way as exuding it like an essence. The darkest undernotes of alcohol. Shaken up in a sudden cocktail of acrid and bitter.

I don't want to imply he was a tramp, or scruffy. There was nothing down at heel about him at all. He was bearded and pale, with a black and white Arab scarf round his neck, though I noticed that only later as he told me his story. There was something distinctive about him. He'd stood out in that crowd at Crewe and I can't quite tell you why. Earring apart I mean. He was different. Even the way of his drunkenness was different. Again I can't explain, other than to say that he'd retained his dignity and a terrible kind of poignancy. His face wore a startled, incredulous mask.

To look at he seemed to be a living contradiction, part hippie, part squaddie. And his tipple was whisky. However well lubricated he already was, there was obviously room for more. Before the girl had trundled the trolley out of our compartment, he was up on his feet again, if uncertainly, coming back with two of those miniature bottles. (I could tell even from the rear, by the girl's whole demeanour and body language that she didn't want to serve him at all.) He drank straight from the bottle. As if it were pop. And his face wore a strange urgency. The rest of us were tame, ordinary. He possessed a dark knowledge it pained him not to share.

I hope he doesn't get too pally, I thought. I felt very stuck, pushed up against the window, half obliterated by my holdall and bag. I was a captive audience.

It was now I saw the nose stud; silver again to match that earring in his left ear. With a kind of diamond in the middle, very bright.

* * * *

'You tell stories don't you?'

I was eight. I was about to be interrogated by Mrs Stannard and I was standing by the back gate with my pet jackdaw on my shoulder.

His name was Coco. I'd bought him for half a crown (a lot of money, that; several weeks' pocket money) from a bigger boy in our school, Alan. He was always hanging round the castle, climbing up on the crumbly walls where the different pinks and dark reds of Aunty Betsy grew in close tufts. There, and on the top of the Watergate tower near the river, jackdaws would gather squabbling and clattering. Sometimes the boys went there with air guns. I didn't ask Alan how he'd got hold of Coco. It was best not to know.

Anyway there I was, the star of the show with this feathered conversation piece on my shoulder and here was the formidable lady herself with her curt question, her accusing air.

'You tell stories don't you?'

'Oh yes. I like telling stories,' I said.

Bizarre as it sounds it was only years later that I realised she was calling me a liar. She must have been disconcerted by my positive response but she didn't show it. Mrs Stannard was nothing if not cool. I'd taken it for granted she was talking quite literally about the stories I told in front of the class for Miss Roberts on Friday afternoons in Free Choice. A shy child most of the time, though not above showing off my tame jackdaw quite shamelessly, I would always burst into narrative life whenever the spirit moved and whenever there were people obliging enough to listen.

But what did Mrs Stannard mean by telling me I told lies?

There was now no way I would ever find out, though the oddness and awkwardness of the encounter stayed with me. Could she could have been told I was a liar by my grandmother, who only the week before had reprimanded me for saying there were hundreds of cats in the garden when there were only two?

But that was exaggeration. Surely a different matter altogether.

Anyway, telling stories isn't telling lies, is it?

So why did those frank German eyes so unsettle me all those years later?

* * * *

I remember little of the journey in terms of looking out of the window. I was too conscious of the man sitting beside me, the whisky quietly disappearing. It was February, the light of rare clarity, the Wirral shore sharply visible.

By the time we'd reached Shotton the whisky was gone. I sensed the man's restlessness immediately, a seething sense of disturbance, a raw energy. Above all a sense of sadness and loss, a negative power.

'I've committed an indiscretion, haven't I?'

His voice was insistent.

Now I'm not one of those people who think it's unwise to enter into conversations with strangers on trains. I felt it would be unwise not to answer, in these circumstances anyway, and on some level I don't understand, I had no choice. I wanted, needed to respond to the man's real anguish. It was tangible.

'What do you mean?'

'Sitting alongside a lady when I'm drunk. I was minding my own business, watching my gear at the back. Didn't want to disturb anyone.'

'It's all right.'

'Is it? I wish it bloody well was. I've got an excuse though. For being drunk like this. I've been travelling for three days. From Kurdistan. Just now touched down at Birmingham and they're sending me to be assessed in this bleeding Welsh place, what's it called, Plas Eryri or something. I'll be seen by these shrinks there.'

I gulped. I'd never heard of Plas Eryri but I could tell him what the words meant.

'Plas Eryri means palace of the eagles.'

'Sounds weird. Have you ever heard of it? It's in Bangor.'

'No,' I said.

Just lowering his voice a fraction he continued. 'It's a post traumatic stress unit.' He looked at me. His eyes were dark brown, anxious. Wearied. I looked at him. The eye contact was prolonged, unnatural.

'If I told you what I've seen in the last few months, well, years, you wouldn't believe me. You'd never guess what I've been doing out there for a start.'

I didn't say anything, just gave him a vague sort of nod.

'I've been doing the kind of crazy job only a drunk like me would do. You've got to be drunk or crazy. Take your pick.'

I was trying not to stare at the brilliant nose stud. He wasn't particularly tall. His dark hair was receding. He had an aura about him. Darkness. Great courage. Sorrow. Then darkness again.

'Out there,' he said, 'You wouldn't believe. Death, destruction. Human life counts for nothing.' He now turned towards me and looked at me very hard.

'I'm not a mercenary.'

'No,' I said.

'Mind, I've had my share of fighting. Ten years in the British army. The Falklands. The Gulf. Northern Ireland. The lot. What've I been doing now? Working in a minefield, that's what.' He laughed. The expression 'hollow laughter' is common enough, but believe me you never heard laughter as hollow as this. 'Out there with a load of stupid buggers who'd have your ... bum blown off as soon as look at you.' He'd meant to say 'balls' but quickly changed the word as a sop to my sensibilities. I was strangely touched.

'Making safe. That's what I've been doing. That's what they call it. Making safe.' He toyed with the two words as if suddenly aware of their meaning. 'Not that you can, and it's a bloody dangerous process even trying. Years from now there'll still be kids, farmers, going up with a bang. Legs missing. Hands missing. You can't make it safe. Safer, maybe.'

Again his eyes probed mine. We were level with a sea wall. Beyond it the Dee estuary was grey wrinkled calm.

'What I've seen .... No one knows what's going on out there. Or cares. These shrinks who'll assess me. Where I'm being sent. What do they know about anything? They've taken away my photographs. Some fella from the foreign office. Took the negatives too ....'

Then came the laughter again. Exhausted hopeless laughter.

* * * *

When I got home I told Jim about my encounter with the man from Kurdistan.

'Was he a Kurd?' Jim asked. A reasonable enough question I suppose.

'No. He was English. A bit of a Midlands accent. He didn't seem to know what was happening except that he was being sent to this Plas Eryri. Have you heard of it?'

'No,' said Jim. 'Sounds to me like someone's been having you on.'

'I'm sure it was true,' I said. 'He'd been doing bomb disposal work. Working in a minefield. It had really got to him. He was in a terrible state.'

'A blind drunk doing bomb disposal work? Pull the other one.'

I stared at him. His face wore a wry, amused look. It's one I know well.

I didn't say anymore.

* * * *

Beep, beep beep, beep, sang the lorries.

The class had gone. All of them. Helga had been the last to leave. She'd written a piece about the embroidery class she'd been attending. As always I was impressed by her industry, her commitment.

I was also sure that beyond the literal truth she always provided there was the capacity for imaginative flights. She denied them though, as if she were afraid. Perhaps she was right to be cautious. Perhaps the dividing line between fact and fiction is not one to be blurred, distorted.

I thought of the man from Kurdistan. I thought about him a lot. Had he been simply spinning me a yarn? What was the nature of the difference between Jim and me in regard to our receptivity? I was inclined to believe people, give them the benefit of the doubt. Jim was an arch sceptic. Always. With him it was automatic. His attitude to life was quizzical, testing. Our marriage only worked because we'd both learned pretty early on to accept that we were never going to be soulmates. We gave ourselves plenty of space. We didn't expect too much.

I don't often dream. They say though, don't they, that we do in fact dream three or four separate dreams every night but for the most part we just don't remember them. Maybe. The night before I'd had a very strange dream indeed.

It started on a train. We were moving through a war-torn landscape. There were burned out tanks. There were bodies. I wasn't afraid, though. Strangely. I felt detached, even relaxed, although I was witnessing horrors, the aftermath of terrible human carnage. Then I got up and calmly walked through to a kitchen, one that seemed slightly familiar but which I couldn't quite place. We weren't on a train anymore. The kitchen was cold and thin with a high ceiling. There were cacti on the windowsill, some very large. I looked at them closely. The more I looked the more bizarre they became. And in the middle of a pale grey-green cactus like a bendy toy Mrs Stannard appeared, surrounded by sprouting scarlet flowers.

'*You tell stories don't you?*' she said.

'No I don't,' I said.

'I'm glad to hear it.' She smiled at me. 'And I don't want to hear any more about it. At all.'

'You won't,' I told her.

I was glad too. I felt a wave of great relief wash over me. Outside the window a girl of about eight or nine appeared. It was Helga, flaxen haired and fiercely plaited. She was offering me a bottle, a very large bottle of whisky.

I moved effortlessly through the glass of the window and sat with Helga on a railway embankment. We were giggling happily, swigging at the bottle. Out of my pocket I took one silver earring, a filigree thing. I fixed it carefully in my ear and then reached for the silver nose stud with the central diamond.

Women of a Certain Age

Puzzling, this ox-bow, if that's what it is. A loop of water, an enclosure of trees just to the left of the road, thin trees growing too closely together. The ribbon of water, scarcely more than a wide clean ditch, is fenced off from the surrounding field. A heron perches on one of the fencing stakes. It looks somehow disreputable, shabby and hunched, its bill sharp yellow against blue-grey.

The heron has all the time in the world.

Driving, Jane could not see the heron, nor the blink of the water like a fish. She hoped they would not ruin all this with the gas terminal; the low-lying fields, reedy and damp, and beyond them the dunes, but she guessed they would. They called it progress. She could not see the house in the far trees either, the pines on the low ridge, the pale gable, but the young man she did see. He meant nothing to her. He would flicker into her life for just this brief moment, and then he'd be gone, carrying one of those artist portfolio things. He'd walked down the sloped field on the right and was standing there, ready to cross the road.

Just for a moment their eyes met. It was September, feeling like summer still, but with a hint of change in it. Jane was old enough now to not want winter, not want the everlasting evenings, the cold and wet, old enough to look appreciatively but with a sense of reminiscence at the young man's shape, the aplomb of youth. He was tanned and slim but nothing spectacular. Why then this strange unbidden stirring? She wriggled and sat up straight, glanced at her watch, put her foot down, firm, on the accelerator.

As the young man crossed the road (and this she did not see, disciplining herself not to look up into the mirror) the heron flapped off, sluggishly half annoyed, creaked and circled, and, for something to do, flew off towards a half-dead willow, a pollard at the corner of the field. The young man took the path alongside the ox-bow, the cramped tanglewood. There was something colourless about him, an absence. The sun had bleached his ordinary brown hair. He wore pale jeans and a white, too-big-for-him shirt, the sleeves rolled up on arms that were just this side of scrawny. He readjusted the large awkwardness of the portfolio under his arm and with his right hand, checked again that he had the packet of condoms in his pocket.

By now the driving woman was approaching the dock at Mostyn, the stacks of timber, the quiet cranes. There was a waiting quality about the place she liked, and there on the right, was The Honest Man, that old pub that intrigued her with its carving above the door, the inscribed date, curvy numerals in revamped plaster. The carving, echoed in the inn sign, again caught her eye; that bearded face, that man, a shepherd, surely a Christ figure, a lamb about his shoulders, hunched into that restricting frame.

Today she'd be continuing with the Metaphysicals, with Donne:

> Batter my heart three person'd God; for you
> As yet but knocke, breathe, shine, and seeke to mend;

Actually I feel quite battered enough as it is, thank you God, she told herself.

* * * *

Towards the house Jane had not been able to see, pale gabled among pines, with its drive of shabby gravel, the young man was walking. He had taken his time, knowing Maura would be watching out for him, knowing and slowing deliberately, not out of any sense of cruelty (he was too detached) but simply secure, even complacent in his awareness of the effect he had on her.

They both knew they'd be saying goodbye, and this long approach over the stubble fields was part of it. It should not be hurried. Perhaps it was the artist in him. He'd crossed the railway, feeling still the palpitation in the hot boards of the crossing just after the Holyhead train zimmed through. He remembered the Burnet moths on the dunes, the hare he'd disturbed in the quaking-grass. Maura knew all the botanical terms. *Briza media* she'd told him it was, but for her the country terms were still the best: eyebright, hoary plantain, sheep's fescue.

She'd been surprised when he told her he had no intention of going to Art School. Never had, actually. She'd merely assumed it. A different generation, hers. Different values, different aspirations. She saw that now.

I'll carry on with my art. (He liked to reassure her on that score.) Of course I will. But I can see better prospects with Modern Languages and Business Studies. More openings.

Yes, was all she'd said. She looked at him, only half-mockingly, loving the sheer self-sufficiency of him.

Did they know? His parents? That he had no intention of coming back? Ever? That awful skinhead brother of his and the girl with the piles of bright orange hair, the black leather and those incongruously delicate little silver chains. They had *style*, all of them in their ghastly way, she conceded. But she'd driven past the run-down estate where he lived, and seen there was no life for him there. Cracked pebble dash and cracked guttering, gardens that weren't gardens at all but fields of tussocks and pram wheels. She would have liked to rescue him from all that but it simply wasn't necessary. He was quite capable of rescuing himself.

OK so what if she was a snob?

Maura'd watched him walking towards the house. He'd certainly taken his time. And watching him like this, from up here in her bedroom, knowing he *knew* she was watching, canny voyeur of his own impact, (cool just wasn't the word), she couldn't stop herself smiling. Was glad that she was so much less the fool than she used to be. Had been able to sum him up at the start, had learned all the tricks, the blocks and evasions, the strategies that were part cynicism, part simple self-defence. She'd been wary, guarded, knowing the score — that time-honoured pattern of older woman and boy on the make.

So why now, as she heard his footsteps, their soft crunch on the drive, did she pour herself this whisky?

* * * *

The seminar went well. The holy sonnets, yes, but Jane wanted them to see how the erotic and the religious were so intertwined, how the language of the one mode, the one meaning, was employed so effectively in terms of the other. The link, of course was the intensity of the experience in each case. Peak experience, if you like. *And yet the body is its boke* ....

Next week, we'll be looking at Andrew Marvell. I want everyone to read 'The Horatian Ode', looking up all the references in the Helen Gardner, and referring to the social context notes I handed out at the start of the course ....

Some of them were keen. Their eyes showed it, and it was for these Jane lived, the shining eyes of those who revelled in the primacy of the word as she did. The rest, the bored, the shuffling ones, she carried as ballast. That was their problem.

It was still hot outside. Sometimes, if she had a little time to kill and no particular pressure, examination papers or whatever, she would drive into Chester. If she could find somewhere to park, way out of the centre it had to be too, in one of those side streets near the canal, she'd walk into town and eat a take-away sandwich in the gardens of the cathedral. Near the Bell Tower there were always tame, pert chaffinches, and occasionally, squirrels. She liked the moving plumes of whispy fluff that were their tails, the delicacy of their movements. Best of all she liked their sharp, feral faces.

Today she was restless. She went into the SPCK shop in Werburgh Street, where there was a book sale, something she found irresistible, and bought a much reduced critical biography of Stevie Smith. Delighted with her bargain as a child might be with an unexpected new toy, she wandered back towards the cathedral. Such dappling light, and for her, such unaccountable lightness of *spirit.* Young was how she felt, young and eager yet, somehow, calm and untroubled too. A rare combination, that.

She wondered if the cloister garden was open. That had been a favourite place, before her marriage and after, but strangely, since the divorce, on the few occasions she'd ventured in she'd always found the heavy door locked against her. It was locked today, too. Why? There's no need to take it personally, she said to herself, pushing her face up against the stained glass, and blinking. *Hortus enclosus*. There was the fountain; there were the pigeons, the seats, the thorn trees, the flagstones and the thin grass, and around and above all these, the rich carved sandstone, towering, of high windows and gargoyles.

But she could not get inside.

* * * *

How vain he was. And if Maura had loved him, him in his entirety, rather than the idea of him, which she could, of course, handle with relish and wry amusement, how it would have irked her.

There was something lacking in him, though, wasn't there? So young and so, what was it? Not shallow, no, he wasn't *shallow* this callow youth of hers, it wasn't that. The lack wasn't quite a lack after all. There was something calculated about everything he did, and, consequently, from her viewpoint, so jaded, so spoiled, there was something refreshing. An absence of feeling, and who was to say that this apparent lack of depth was not a new form of depth in its own right? A sign of the times. Whatever it was, it was good. It kept her safe.

Knowing this was not only goodbye, but that time was there in abundance for them, with Charles in Strasbourg till Tuesday at least, and with not even the slightest possibility (thank God!) of his unexpected return, Maura lavished attention on him. It was a game, this. So she let the first time be vigorously brief and somewhat perfunctory. Things could only improve.

Afterwards they half sat, half lay on the bed, on the apple green duvet among plump white cushions, and Maura flicked through his most recent sketches. These were not by any means up to his usual standard, and she told him so.

I know, he said.

Unsaid, but clear to both of them, was the simple fact that he didn't much care. He was on the verge of a creating a new self to live in, far from here. It was a sideline at the moment, all this art stuff. Talent he had, but genius, whatever that self-consuming thing might be, was not in evidence. Nor did he want it to be.

You got the *soul* of the dunes, though, she said, with a theatrical hint of sadness, seeing again the vistas he'd created last winter. Wash of cold sky, hint of east wind in marram, whirligig of sand.

I never got yours, did I?

Soul? My soul? Do you believe in souls, then?

I don't think I do, really. Sorry. To disappoint you.

Don't pretend to be sorry. You're far too hard-headed to believe in anything so *whispy*, aren't you? But I did, you know. Believe. You'd be surprised. I used to be very into soul and *weltschmertz*. That sort of thing.

There was a new note in her voice he didn't like. To silence her he pulled her over to him. She was so lithe, neat was the word for her, yes, neat. You would not have thought she was the mother of twin daughters three years his senior, and born into very different circumstances. Planned and welcomed and provided for. Groomed for stardom, you might say.

Just then the heron flew back to the ox-bow and the fence. It just sat there. It just waited and watched.

* * * *

Then, as Jane turned away from the garden door, she saw the paintings. Children's paintings; kids from local primary schools. Of Chester and the cathedral. For the Festival. They were good. Really good. And some were batiks. Were they for sale? They were full of detail and exuberance.

How strange was the effect of the slanting sun, coming in from the garden through stained glass, playing rainbows on the old stone of the cloisters. She sat on the cold bench along the wall as the coloured light trembled over her. She felt swimmy in this puzzle, this jigsaw of fractured light, sitting bolt upright now against the hardness of the wall, as if its physicality, its sheer materiality, the unyieldingness of it, could brace her, but fidgeting, definitely, fumbling in her handbag for his letter. She'd read it, sort of, when it arrived this morning, but only while gulping her coffee and grabbing her toast.

Now she would read it properly. Savour, slow savour of words. And meanings.

She'd thought he was a widower. They'd met at a lecture on the Mystery Plays three months ago. Over a cup of insipid coffee they'd exchanged inconsequential notes on their various experiences of Lincoln Cathedral, of Bath Abbey, of Avebury, of the Rollright Stones. He didn't know quite what he believed in, he'd said, but there was something, he was sure, had to be. Perhaps he could be described as a Buddhist of sorts. I'm a lapsed Welsh Calvinistic Methodist myself, she'd told him, giggling almost, unaccountably. He was so easy to talk to.

She just assumed he was a widower. It was nothing he said, but wouldn't he have been there with his wife, if he had one? When Jane finally heard about her, some weeks and several meetings later, she was, to put it mildly, surprised. Not that she was incapable of having an affair. He was, admittedly, a good deal older than she was, but that didn't matter. She just felt, sadly, that he was too proper, too old-fashioned, to contemplate one. Since the divorce she'd had her share of flings. Well, two, actually, and flings she only called them retrospectively. She'd had higher hopes at the time. Now she saw those amorous escapades had been necessary as ego-boosts, had been important in that they'd proved she could still attract. That's all.

This was different. Yet, paradoxically, because she respected him, she hadn't wanted to appear, well, flighty. Had, in fact, been ultra correct. Now, in his letter, he was telling her, taking his courage in both hands. He quoted Donne. Today, of all days, Donne!

> I wonder by my troth, what thou and I did
> till we lov'd? were we not wean'd till then?

He was coming to see her this evening. He was coming to

her poky, cluttered flat in what had once been the Rectory. She consoled herself that the clutter was of the kind that he, the lover of books, would savour, along with the prints and the blue lacquered bowls she collected, the ceramic owls, and, best of all perhaps, the glass one that sat on the wide white window sill. It didn't always happen of course, but just sometimes its sharp facets would catch the evening sun. Then it became one entire topaz flame.

Bubble

Then it was winter and all the long bleached benches outside the Surfers' Diner disappeared. Gone were the deep bistro-style coffee cups, the gingham tablecloths, the salty pennants in the wind, and for Clare, stuck at her perch, the cash desk in the window of The Golden Plaice on the corner, gone was the summer of her life, just like that, overnight, gone, never to return.

'I didn't want a diet Pepsi, Duncan,' whined a thin blonde nearby. 'Take it back and get me the ordinary.'

And the mild-mannered Duncan took it back and got her the ordinary, only to find her complaining that she hadn't brought her sun cream, and here she was with a red patch right across the bridge of her nose and it was sure to peel, and you didn't expect that in September and why wasn't Duncan listening?

Why doesn't Duncan tell her to shut up, Clare thought. It was quiet, very quiet, so Clare left the cash desk and came down into the body of the café and started emptying the ashtrays and giving all the tables a lick and a promise with a cloth that smelled strongly of pine disinfectant. It was something to do. She was not only bored. She was angry. Why did her father have to squeeze the season dry like this every time? As far as Clare was concerned the Surfers' Diner had the right idea. As soon as the official school holidays were over that was it, but oh no, that was far too simple for Dad, who kept going at weekends for the occasional stray holiday-maker until it was downright embarrassing.

Clare was at that age when having parents of any kind at all is embarrassing, but to have the kind of father who took it upon himself to uphold standards (as he was at pains to tell everyone) single-handedly, who thought nothing of going into the diner and complaining about the noise from the juke-box, and the cars revving up outside, well, Clare just wished the earth would open up and swallow her sometimes.

She wouldn't have minded it being quiet like this if she'd been able to kid herself she could still dream about Clyde, and pretend things might just work out after all. But she knew, realistically, that it hadn't and it wouldn't, and the summer of her life had been almost an unmitigated disaster. There had been Clyde though, and even if she had ruined it all by bursting into tears in the back of the car after the barbecue so that he brought her home, which was humiliating, and the more kind he was the more humiliating it became, well, he must have fancied her to start with, so there had to be hope. What she wanted to know was whether she'd always be frigid like that. She'd talked it over in some detail with Jane and Ceri, who tried to reassure her and said it was all because she'd got herself into such a state of anticipation, that she was all in a tremble of feverpitch excitement, and it could have gone either way. So she shouldn't worry. Everything would be OK in the end.

Meanwhile the thin blonde was whining her way through a knickerbocker glory. Clare decided that the long-suffering Duncan was quite nice looking really, so she started to look at him in the fixed half-asleep-through-your-eyelashes way Jane had taught her, just to see what happened, and he actually blushed, poor thing. To crown this moment of glory, Clare walked past their table with her high-powered disinfected cloth and hovered there, brazen as you like, while Duncan went redder and redder and Whining Blonde delved obliviously into the deepest reaches of her sundae glass. What more might Clare have made of this conquest had her father not repeatedly glowered at her, his head bobbing up above the top of the fryer and between the rowed bottles of brown fruity sauce?

'Can I go now, Dad?' she asked at last. Surely he wasn't going to be so stupid as to stay open till the bitter end again?

'Have you wiped all the tables?'

'Yes.'

'You've got a gallon of that stuff on the cloth, again, haven't you? I don't want this place to smell like a clinic. I keep telling you. Have you checked the cutlery?'

'Yes, Dad.'

'You can go when you've mopped up in the back, I suppose. You've told your mother where you're going?'

'Dad, where else would I be going but Ceri's? You know quite well, so why make such a thing of it?'

'It's only right I should check.'

'Yes Dad.'

Clare sighed, and after the required mopping, she made her way heavily upstairs to the flat. Her mother, who been on duty in the café till mid-afternoon was now testing her pronunciation with her Welsh cassettes. Her accent was atrocious but nobody could deny her persistence. Clare was convinced that part, at least, of her eagerness to learn the language and immerse herself in the culture of her adopted homeland, was due to the fact that, here, at last, was a way to assert her independence from her husband.

When Brian had been made redundant four years ago, she hadn't wanted him to invest his severance lump sum in a fish restaurant, for heaven's sake, in an outlandish place in the middle of nowhere, in Wales, where he'd once, just once, come for a holiday as a child. She wasn't consulted. But by the time she'd been there a few months, and they seemed about to make a go of it, she decided she'd learn something about the country she was living in. For a start she was intrigued by the books Clare was bringing home from school. OK, Brian didn't like it. Tough. She more than pulled her weight in the café, so he couldn't in all fairness complain about how she spent her spare time.

This was something else, her own province, and he with his prejudices, and his absurdly old-fashioned suspicion of what his father before him had called 'book-learning', could lump it. Brian had frowned a lot, looked decidedly sulky in fact, but mostly said nothing and, no doubt in revenge as he saw it, (though neither his wife nor his daughter regretted his absence) spent more and more of his time at the golf club.

With the closing of the Surfers' Diner all the colour had gone out of the place. Not that much surfing was actually ever done here, it had to be said, though after a television feature film a few years back, the small resort had experienced a brief renaissance, and there was no denying the magnificence of the Atlantic rollers on those rare occasions when the winds and the tides were just right. Still, however inauthentic the diner's clientele might be, they lent a certain raffish glamour to the street of souvenir shops, the rows of grey stone cottages, now mostly rented out as summer homes. Clare was into style in a big way and these people certainly had tons of it. She loved to watch the all bronzed torsos, the bright shirts and sawn-off frayed denims. She loved listening to the leggy girls with their high pitched laughter. However much her father might object, she relished the blare of car radios, the strong sweet smell of burnt caramel and Mississippi Mud Pie, the assignations, that whole atmosphere of manic abandon. If it was a brittle, contrived brightness Clare was not to know how precarious it was, how much a bubble. For her, now the summer was over, the blueness of the sky and this sudden freak heat only mocked the greyness, the uniform drabness of the village by the sea.

Saturday night, and how dead it all was. Clare washed quickly and changed, and then with a murmur to her mother, who kept interrupting the voice on the tape with her own strangled vowels, something to do with the delights of a traditional *noson lawen*, she was off up the road and out of the village, through the lane with its tall hedges to Ceri's house. The sky in the west over the bay was streaked pink and golden with sunset and Clare was so glad to be out she kept breathing in great gulps of cool air. It was just as she was about to cross the road that she noticed the car parked further up on the right, and a young man walking towards her.

It was Clyde. She couldn't believe it. He'd been down for his last weekend three weeks ago. He'd said so. What was he doing here now?

'Clare,' he said. 'I'm so glad to see you. I've waited ages on the off chance you'd be coming this way.'

Then, incredulous, she listened as he told her about the trouble he was in, how the police were after him, and how it wasn't *that* serious, but ....

'What have you done?' Clare demanded, never one to be satisfied with vagueness. She'd never seen her hero like this, a dwindled figure, unshaven, furtive-looking. Already the tan was fading to an unattractive sallowness.

'They're after me and some of the others for, well, just supplying a bit of speed now and then, nothing heavy.'

'Amphetamines?'

'Yes.'

'How did you ever get into anything like that? What's going to happen? Are they going to arrest you? What are you doing here?'

When it came to interrogation Clare was in a class of her own, and actually giving Clyde a chance to answer didn't seem important.

'They've pulled Jason and Dave in for questioning. I thought I could just lie low for a bit. Sally's given me the key to her parents' caravan, so I'm up at the Penrhos site and ....'

'Yes?'

'I haven't got any money, Clare. I was wondering ....'

'But Clyde, you'll have to go back eventually, won't you? You can't go into hiding, like a wanted man or something. This isn't the wild west is it?'

'No.'

Clare was conscious that she was nagging in a peculiarly middle-aged way. This was all wrong. Clyde was older than she was. What was he, twenty something? She felt he should have more sense. What sort of game was he playing?

'What about your job?'

'I just went into a kind of panic, I suppose. I just got into my car and drove. I couldn't think of anywhere else to go, so I came here.'

'You're supposed to be at work?'

'I was working yesterday. I heard about the others being pulled in last night and as soon as I heard I just got away as fast as I could.'

'You've got to be back on Monday, though, haven't you, Clyde? If you're not you'll blow *everything*.'

Then, suddenly, he seemed to crumple in front of her. It was excruciating. She didn't know where to look. 'Hell, Clare. What am I going to do?'

'Go back,' she said firmly. 'What do your parents think? Do they know?'

'They don't know anything. I've got my own flat and I hardly ever see them anyway. I haven't even got money for the petrol home.'

'Well, I've only got the money I'm saving to go skiing with the school at Christmas. I've been really looking forward to that, but look, I can let you have £20, just so you can get back. But you've got to promise you will go back. You promise, right? I mean, what else can you do?'

'Nothing,' he said numbly.

It was awful. He looked so small, so pathetic, and as utterly unromantic as anyone possibly could. All Clare's illusions were collapsing at her feet, literally, and this brought out her practical streak with a vengeance.

'You wait here,' she said. 'I'll go home. I'll have to make some excuse though. I'll say I'm going to lend Ceri my new CD, and I'll bring you the money. Then you can drive back to Derby and face up to whatever happens. Running away is just stupid, Clyde. You know it is.'

Then Clare was off, striding down the lane with what seemed to Clyde an excess of intimidating energy. She felt calm and uncluttered, as if a great wave was bowling her along, leaving in her wake the ghost of a beach boy for whom there was simply nothing left to do but sit quietly in his car in the deepening shadows and wait for her return.

Snatchings of Guilty Time

'Write,' said the grave young man, and his words were equal and simple as pebbles, 'from what you know, but not as the outside everyday world knows it.'

(Not, then, the outside everyday world ... but the inside, extraordinary.)

The grave young man sits in the window. Outside plumes of pampas grass are waving. The garden contains still, sheltered here in its island cup, the colours of late autumn. Snowberries and kaffir lilies, cinnamon leaves like small gilt brooches.

'Write from the inside,' says the grave young man, 'from your perceptions, from the wisdom of all that sensory knowledge your body holds.'

(Ah, how very Laurentian, thinks Meg. She chews her pen, looking out through the wide window, evading his eyes.)

There are Scots pines. Five of them. A silver birch with the shimmer of a Roman candle. There is a path of irregular flat stones set askew. It crosses a lawn; ragged edges, scatterings of brown wet leaves. A summer house on the far side of the island, open to the water.

'But write about *what*?' asks the fussy man, balding. Houndstooth check tweed jacket, a hint, noticed yesterday evening over coffee, of halitosis.

'About anything you like,' says the earnest girl, her indignation tangible. People are just not receptive enough, but she will receive and respond. She'll show them all.

Meg sighs for her. Exasperation and who knows what pent-up forces emanate from her. A hank of greasy hair, bitten-down-to-the-quick fingernails where pink new skin tries to grow again. And such intolerance. Meg can't remember her name. Strange, but not really when you think about it. Last night when they were introduced, she found she couldn't concentrate, too much to take in for one day, the long journey by train, the jostle of them as they arrived, some with her, picked up from the station at Bangor, others by car. There were only seven of them but it felt like more.

What am I doing here, she found herself asking.

The girl bites her underlip. Fussy man, Balding asks if they can describe what they see through the window.

'Of course,' their tutor runs a hand through his fine straight hair. The girl bridles.

Child, because you *are* still a child, Meg observes, which is why that obvious suggestion so annoys you, you are impatient with your life, your self, with everything. There's a fever in you.

Beyond the rocks, invisible from here, moored boats are jangling their choppy music. As the wind rises the sound of all that ringing grows fierce, is orchestrated. One highpitched whine of a note, one banshee call, lifts seven heads, all startled. Pens held in hands, seven masks of puzzlement turn towards him, their grave young man who sits in the window, his back to the glow of the garden, the straits, the sharp light.

His name is Simon, their tutor, their guide and mentor. But he does not know this place.

At once he acknowledges the fact. It's as if Meg has caught his thought processes, their uncertain quickness. He looks at them, wondering how the week will gell, how they'll operate, these seven strangers and himself, this group of people drawn together to write, to wield words. English words on a Welsh island, that is not quite an island, that has seen in turn so many invaders come and go. And sometimes stay.

'I wonder what the history of this place is.' He moves sideways along the window seat, only too pleased to allow Fussy man, Balding as much view of outside as he wants. It is a handsome room, the wide window rare in a house this old. But of course this must be an extension. 'It will have its own tales to tell.'

'Angelsey was the last bastion of the druids,' says the American postgraduate student, the anthropologist named Chuck. Now Meg has remembered *his* name, an exploded cliché. No one ever looked less like a Chuck, though that Polish-sounding surname does fit him. He has the most arresting face. Those high cheek bones might betray a Slav origin. But could just as easily be Cherokee. Meg is amused at the way she's slotting all these people into imaginary pigeonholes.

She thinks and sits. Is conscious of the breathing of the seven others around her. Is conscious of her own breathing, measured, at ease.

* * * *

Write from the inside — was what Simon said — *from your perceptions, from the wisdom of all that sensory knowledge your body holds.*

But she does not want to look inside, afraid of what she might find. She has come here to escape from herself.

What, instead, could this place tell her? She turns to gaze across the straits where dark mountains climb, sees a thin blade of white, a waterfall, a long thread against a green that is almost black. Someone over there might be looking across the straits too, over here at us, at just this moment. Chuck's bony face appears in her mind's eye. She hears the laid back slur of his accent. Druids and Romans.

Fragments, floodings of sound. A stream, a small river where white pebbles gather. Meg is far away, moving in a mythic landscape. An army bristles and waits on the mainland shore. It is A.D. 60. Suetonius Paulinus stands and looks across to

Mona, refuge of insurrectionists. Of infamous tribal priests. He swims his cavalry across. Imagine them, the horses struggling to find their feet, the men, the best of Rome and battle seasoned, dreading still whatever truth might fix itself to tales they've heard. Golden sickles slicing a music of their own out of what ritual? Human sacrifices. Sacred groves.

Even the most sceptical tremble. Just a little. Now the infantry embark from their flat-bottomed boats as they scratch and grate in the shallows, legionaries shouting raucously to each other to keep up their spirits. A huddle of plaid-wrapped figures watch from a bluff.

Meg walks on her own in the garden. At this end the lawn is mossy. Recent rain has brought about a sudden sprouting of tiny toadstools, spindly frail orangey brown things. Long stems, fluted tops.

It is her sixtieth birthday. Funny, isn't it, how birthdays lose significance, how little they come to matter, except as landmarks of time slithering past and away from you. Think of all that childhood excitement. Those solemn announcements — I'm six and a half; I'm seven and threequarters — don't cheek your elders, I'm older than you.

I'm older than all of you, thinks Meg. Amongst these strangers she will say nothing about her birthday. She will keep it to herself, as a Roman soldier keeps his fear.

Only a month ago life had seemed normal. She woke on what should have been an ordinary morning, an ordinary day. She shifted comfortably in their bed, half reaching out to Edward at her side.

He can't be cold, he can't be dead.

Busy, bustling, plenty to do till after the funeral. Then the great hollowness. I can't stand this emptiness, Meg thought. I'll go mad if I can't fill this emptiness.

Quite by chance, she spotted a brochure in the library. She'd gone to change her books, those books she took out dutifully to read only mechanically; eyes scanning pages, gleaning next to nothing.

WRITE ON AN ISLAND

enjoy

inspiring scenery
congenial company
expert tuition

— but of course it wasn't quite an island. Among all the information about the course and the prize-winning, much published poet (she'd never heard of him) who would be their tutor, there was a description of the 'island' itself, and photographs. One showed it at full tide, lapped delightfully by moody water, another with the water gone, the causeway revealed with its garnish of seaweed. I shall bring my new walking boots, she said to herself. That looks slippery.

As a child she'd always written. As soon as she could string words together she shaped small poems, kept them in a big scrapbook with pictures she liked, postcards, cuttings from papers. Animals were her favourites. And aerial views, rare then, and one, the very best of all, the castle of Ludwig, that mad king of Bavaria. So much the fairy castle it looked untrue.

Leaving school she'd worked for seven years in the tax office, the scrapbook bundled to the back of a cupboard, forgotten about. Then came marriage to Edward, three children, and latterly the occasional bed and breakfast guest. She'd always read widely but the writing, until a few years ago, had stopped. When those snatchings of guilty time were resumed they gave her real pleasure. Meg wrote descriptively, of moods, of skies, of people's faces. Of the bustle in the market. Of the stillness around the great minster when all the tourists were gone, a gleaming sense of time hanging there, with the last of the leaves on the beeches. And this place?

Now she was actually supposed to write she perversely felt she didn't want to. She'd been given permission, so why didn't it all flow? She wished she could be here on her own, to simply sit and watch and do nothing. Just follow the moods of weather on the straits, shifts of light on the mountains.

It was all too much of an effort lately. Everything.

* * * *

I must stop calling him Fussy Man, Balding, Meg tells herself. His name is Gus. She is sitting with the others again, in those deep sink-you-comfortably chairs, for a review of the day's work. They've all had to write something about the atmosphere of the island.

'That's the starting point. Let it lead you wherever you want to go. Think of Klee taking a line for a walk.'

Again Simon is sitting in the window with his back to the light, the sunset behind him. Glitter reflects back from the water, is gilding the bark of the Scots pines.

She knows them all now. Earnest Girl is Jodie Carpenter. An exuberant-sounding name which doesn't suit her, but strangely perhaps she seems to grow into her name, has washed her lank hair for a start which has transformed itself into a fluffy dark nimbus about her face. When she smiles (as now, for instance, in catching Chuck's eye) she is almost pretty. There are the sisters, Delia and April. You wouldn't take them for sisters but once you know, you see similarities in build, in the shape of the head. Colouring too, but Delia, the elegant one, younger, dominant, uses make-up expertly. The more dowdy April has put too much blusher on her cheekbones. She looks like a doll, but weary.

What are they all doing here? Though Meg *does* write she can't pretend that's why she's here, really. It was her young raw widowhood brought her.

Delia teaches English in a sixth form college, is perhaps on the look-out for teaching tips. April, Meg guesses, would never have come here without a push from Delia. But who can tell, perhaps Delia needs April more than April needs her. Relationships are such funny things. Not necessarily what they appear to be on the surface.

This may be Wales but there's only one Welsh person present. Emlyn has won a literary prize. The course is part of it, along with a word-processor and a generous book-token. He's a first year theology student. Meg senses his restless intelligence. He and Chuck seem to need to compete with each other, but do so with good grace. Chuck is really into druids, no doubt about it. Has studied shamanism. Ah, thinks Meg, the Cherokee ....

Lastly there's David. A chiropodist. Early forties. By far the quietest of the party, he is proud of his culinary skill. Last night he was on the rota to prepare the evening meal, producing a sumptuous lemon cream, some sort of cross between a syllabub and a mousse. Delicious. But Meg has to invent a background for him, since he's revealed nothing at all: a mid life crisis complete with cheating wife and rebellious teenage sons. She's surprised at the way her thumbnail sketches blossom, grow, would like to know how near they touch reality.

But it is her turn to read.

When the Romans were gone the island was left smouldering.

There had been a grove of yews, ancient trees, their dense heartwood grained red like slabs of meat. Across the near water smoke from a village rose, a deeper sudden smoke with a low flame centre.

If they were all dead, where could the boy go? He had served Geras and Geras had been slaughtered there on the shore, his web of magic no match for a javelin, nor the short ragged bludgeonings that followed. Surely others had survived. Somewhere. He'd hidden, had been lucky. Folk near him, barely yards away, had been dragged from their hiding place. He'd heard their screams. How had the soldiers missed him? They'd been scouring the island for days, had grown slapdash maybe. Was he the last one?

The ground underfoot was still warm. There was rich silver ash everywhere, twisted black twigs, like tangled thread. He sat on the rocks facing the mountains. There were plumes of white smoke. Geras had only just begun to teach him, that was the worse thing. He knew nothing. He who'd waited, who'd wished so fiercely to be a druid himself, who'd felt at last that he was beginning to prove his worthiness, was left now only with inklings of powers beyond him, out of range, receding.

Did all their wisdom go?

'I'm just trying to find my way around in it,' said Meg.

Gus spoke up. 'D'you feel this was a violent place? I don't. For me it's just so incredibly peaceful.'

Gus had been a quantity surveyor with a big construction company. He'd been made redundant a few months earlier. Are we all escaping from something? Are we all at a crossroads, not knowing which road to take?

'It's peaceful now, certainly,' says Meg. 'But it wasn't always. There was something powerful here a long time ago. It was destroyed but it wants to come back.'

'Hey,' said Chuck. 'Are you getting this kinda mediumistic feeling?'

I wish I hadn't started this, thought Meg, glad it was tonight she'd be preparing the evening meal with Emlyn. Peeling onions would be a good cure for a case of, well, whatever would you call it, a haunting?

* * * *

Meg had not cried for Edward. The place where tears came from was blocked. She knew though, that she needed, wanted to cry for him. She'd stayed for a few days with her daughter in Leicester. The house was full of the new life of the grandchildren Meg loved dearly, but whose sheer vividness she could not take. It was too much. Their noise, their fast movement appalled her. She was meant to stay a week but stayed only three days. Her sons had asked her to visit them too, and meant it, but Meg always felt ill at ease with both her daughters-in-law. They were so modern, juggling careers and children with apparent ease. She felt heavy and unbearably old in their presence.

Here, though, aged sixty, secretly, she felt young, untrammelled. It was the relish of being in the company of complete strangers. She could be utterly different, play any kind of role, pretend, experiment. And after this week was over it wouldn't matter.

We're ships that pass in the night, she thought. It's liberating. We won't see each other again.

On the fourth night she couldn't sleep. Her room was on the ground floor, and she'd left the curtains open so she could watch the sky. A half moon came and went among rag clouds and the tide was in. Meg could hear its slipslap sound on the causeway. The nameless boy she'd written about was very clear in her mind.

He'd come back to a burnt island. Geras was dead, he knew that, so why return? Perhaps this was simply a place where he'd been happy, but there was more to it than that. He came back for a purpose. There must have once been a shrine here; where the summer house was now — that was the place. Meg had a momentary vision of a bowl of beaten metal, of strong hands carving out a pattern on wax. There was a sweet resinous scent. She fell into a fitful sleep and dreamed of trees, of a glade with white stones set in a circle, a figure lurking there. But lurking was the wrong word, implying evil intentions. This being, whatever it was, belonged here, was a nurturing spirit. In her dream she strained her eyes to see but the figure faded. Only the boy remained. He was dressed in a rough tunic and breeches wrapped round with thongs. He had something like moccasins on his feet. Somewhere a deep metallic sound echoed. Everywhere there was a singed, acrid smell.

She woke at half past six, suddenly, vibrantly, aware of an almost frantic eagerness. I'll go out, she thought. I won't disturb anyone. She breathed in, half expecting woodsmoke, then crept very quietly on the stepping stones across the lawn, aware of the swish of waves, the melancholy call of sea birds.

There were people in the summer house. She heard voices, light voices with laughter in them. Then Simon and David appeared, thinking themselves alone, each with his arm about the other. They faced her, looked sheepish, embarrassed.

'Good morning,' Meg said clearly. The two men muttered a greeting in return, looked at her and then, shyly, looked back again at each other. A new brave Meg took charge of the situation.

'Love,' she said, 'makes the world beautiful. And this place's special for other reasons too. I don't know what its secret is, but it's got one.'

'You're right. It's a special place,' said Simon, smiling. He seemed to have lost all his gravity. David nodded. He kept his face so totally under control. Meg watched the two of them walk back to the house.

She sat in the summer house in the chilly morning air. The light grew and grew. The sun shone on the mountains across the water, on the boats gently shifting on their moorings. Today there was no wind. She thought of all the people in the house, seeing April making black coffee for Delia and herself, pouring out two bowls of muesli; of Gus, who, last night, aware perhaps of his breath, reeked strongly of peppermint; of Chuck rhythmically beating on his shaman's drum or teasing Emlyn about his word processor from which he was already virtually inseparable. Then there was earnest Jodie of the dark moods, the angry interchanges, and David who'd said so little, seeming to merge with his surroundings. Finally there was Simon, their grave young man, sitting in the window and flicking his hand through his straight hair.

I'd never have bracketed those two together, Meg thought. I suppose I'm really very conventional.

She thought of the boy she'd imagined, if indeed she could have imagined a face so expressively poignant, or a presence so strong. Geras had a name, but he had not. Where had he gone from here? Why was the sense of his being here still so strong?

For the first time since reaching out that morning and finding Edward cold to her touch, Meg cried silently.

The tide was going out now. She knew that on the other side of the island the causeway was revealed again, the water lapping against it with a regular motion.

The Trouble

'The trouble with you,' he'd said, long ago, and more savagely, perhaps, than he'd intended, 'is you've never accepted the world as it is.'

This time it was a young blackbird.

It was fluttering along the pavement in front of her, but fluttering implies a more butterfly-like movement and this was ungainly, a plain awkward fluttering. A large late summer juvenile it was, not yet able to fly but almost adult size. Brown in colour, a special medley of browns ranging from buff to downy golden and including that rather nondescript almost grey brown thrushes wear.

She saw all these things with her artist's eye, and then with a painful tenderness that was not the same thing at all.

Momentarily in her painting she would find the right kind of detachment and from it would grow one of those luminous preternaturally sensitive worlds, a fragment of an old allotment, ugly things you might think, a stove-in watering can, a rusting hoe, viewed with what felt like love but was really precision, an extremity of clear-eyed seeing. Aesthetic distancing, a critic had once told her with a suppressed hiccough over the brim of his glass, is a kind of murderousness.

Now, as she looked down at the blackbird's tell-tale fluttering at her feet, she felt she knew what he meant. She'd experienced the equivalent of a most subtle gear-change, had moved to a different mode, from being outside the blackbird, aware of its movements, curious, but not too perturbed as to what these movements meant, conscious of the gradations of hue in its feathers and admiringly observant, to a condition of sudden raw concern. From the inside. From the point of view that was empathy. As the bird's wings opened she saw that in its back there was a red hole. The fluttering was not the tentative attempt to fly she'd thought it was, rather the desperate attempt of a wounded creature to find safety.

Poor thing, she thought, but wordlessly. Are there thoughts without words? It was more an action than a thought, anyway, this simultaneous process of moving forward, this clutching gesture. How to describe it? An instinct of a kind, perhaps quite involuntary, involving nonetheless an impressive chain reaction of complex neurological impulses. She wanted to help. It was as simple and as complicated as that. Imagination, the capacity to enter the blackbird's experience, that played its part, along with her social conditioning, those nurturing maternal qualities thought of as essentially feminine but by no means the exclusive preserve of that sex. And simply being who she was, of course, that, too, made her reach out and lean down on that particular August morning — that unique mixture of happenstance out of which Joy Harkness emerged. Friend of stray cats, lost dogs and lame ducks, and, well, yes, blackbirds, fighting bitterness for her children's sake, trying, often with difficulty, to live up to the promise of her name.

Does having that most positive and bubbly of names — Joy — create a special sense of responsibility to be happy and helpful at all times? Such a name can so easily become a burden. Joys shouldn't whinge and moan should they, and if they do let the side down and indulge themselves, don't they just feel like hell afterwards? This Joy, I suppose, had got pretty used to her name by now, and pretty used to circumstances that were not exactly one hundred per cent joyful one hundred per cent of the time.

Back to the blackbird.

It was not to know that this towering human (Joy was actually a modest five foot two) was friend rather than foe. How could it? It lurched on, panicky now. Joy half grabbed the small flutterer, the energetic hopping propensities of which proved it to be quite intact. It squawked in pain or fear or both and she didn't have the nerve to hang on, afraid of hurting it further. It scuttled, flapping, to the edge of the pavement where it met the loose lattice-work of some elderly garden fencing. To Joy's astonishment, (how did it manage such a last dash and such a concentrated wriggle?) it somehow squeezed through, falling, then, amongst tangled stems of leggy buddleia into a long garden.

It was quite out of reach.

* * * *

Joy would not describe herself as squeamish. She was a dab hand with the first aid kit whenever one of the children, or even Our Hero himself was hurt, but this incident had got to her. It was just the last straw. She dumped her shopping against the garden lattice work, beyond which the blackbird was presumably still fluttering and would go on doing so till a cat finished it off. She stared at her big handsome National Trust tote bag with its Jacobean design and at the arrangement of bulging plastic carriers. She often did this zooming in on things as a means of steadying herself when things got too much. Again it was the artist's trick, to isolate objects, see them in terms of form, of colour, as arrangements of light and shade, of line and texture. It was a defence mechanism. It distanced her, turning emotions which were difficult to deal with into objective appraisal. To say, though, that the supposedly blithe Joy was now anything other than angry and exasperated would be mincing words.

Today had started off with a warning, an early eight o'clock in the morning telephone call from Our Hero himself, saying he'd be in the area tomorrow and would take the girls out for an hour or two. That wouldn't have mattered really if it hadn't been for the fact that Abbie, an old school friend, was coming to stay for the weekend, and Joy wasn't sure how to handle even the thought of the two of them there together. I should take a course in assertiveness training she said to herself. I should have simply said it wasn't convenient. Still she knew how much her daughters loved to see their father, and Our Hero's proverbial charm was in operation, as ever, in his brief telephone call. She wondered what Abbie would have to say to Stephen while he was there, and more to the point, what she would have to say about him after he'd gone. And what would she think of their peculiar not-really-married-anymore marriage?

Abbie'd be arriving tonight, hence the loads of shopping. It was always better to have too much food in than too little, wasn't it?

Joy always wanted to laugh out loud when she turned over that impressive title, Dr Abigail Jones, in her mind. They'd been friends at school and it was hard to think of scatty, pretty Abbie as a doctor. Joy was frankly relieved that the likelihood of ever being at the receiving end of Abbie's ministrations was decidedly slim. She was safely ensconced in Cardiff somewhere. No, that wasn't fair. Abbie, Joy was sure, would be a very fine doctor indeed. It was just that with their having been friends ever since those still clear memories of infants' sand and water days, Joy could easily think of Abbie incongruously as six years old again; both of them six years old in Abbie's garden amongst the tangled remains of Abbie's brother's home-made kite, which Joy, very naughtily, had persuaded her friend to 'borrow'; both of them crying inconsolably in the knowledge of the anger to come, and the realisation that they'd made a mess of a very special thing.

As it happened this long planned and often postponed visit

was something Joy'd looked forward to for ages. She'd also looked forward, in a much more ambivalent and worrying sort of way, to Our Hero's next appearance, had found herself half hoping he'd be able to stay over a couple of nights, at arm's length, admittedly, in one of those tall narrow bed and breakfast places on the sea front, that they'd spend a little time in each other's company, that it would go well. It was a pipe dream, of course, and as pointless as it was painful. Joy was the saddest of creatures in this respect. It was she who wanted the separation, she who'd used her father's legacy to buy this house at the edge of a marsh near the sea, a place of skies and air and opennesss. True, she could no longer accept Stephen's philandering, but the charm that was as natural as breathing to him, still worked on her, and would, if the other reasons for her discomfort were known, work on Abbie too.

As for Anne and Sally, teenagers now; they still loved their father but were clear-eyed and philosophical about his faults. Joy wished she could be like that. Strange that both her daughters could already give her lessons in mature acceptance. They seemed to know how to operate in that actual factual world where real life dramas are played out. Often Joy felt they were so much more grown up than she was. Pragmatists, the pair of them.

'It's your artistic temperament, Joy, that's what it is,' her mother would say, annoyingly, arriving by train at the dusty summer station, seeing immediately how unhappy she was. Seeing right through that brittle smiling mask. 'You still love him, don't you, my dear, silly girl.' And Joy didn't answer.

* * * *

Sometimes Joy would set Stephen a little test, one that he'd invariably fail, giving her a frisson of bitter satisfaction.

'Come and see what I've done lately,' she'd say. He'd follow her into the studio.

'I like this,' he'd say, picking up one of her more conventional things, even, perhaps, one of those chocolate boxy landscapes she produced for the run of the mill summer visitors. These paintings weren't churned out any old how, she'd always defend herself. She spent a good deal of time on them. But there was no denying they were second best.

Then she'd choose one then that she particularly rated.

'It's a bit bare, isn't it?' he'd say. And he'd smile his still boyish smile. It was so predictable she felt unkind, invisibly manipulating him like this, though Stephen was always unaware of the test taking place. Our Hero, she thought. Even the name she slyly called him was cruel, wasn't it? When had all this cynicism, this sarcasm, begun?

The answer was not hard to find. Having a husband like Stephen, whose womanising was known to everyone around, had caused Joy such pain. The unkindness, as she dubbed it, was another defence mechanism of sorts. Now the thought of Abbie and Our Hero together again came to mind. Yes, he'd been at school with them too, and a tripartite reunion was not what Joy'd envisaged at all.

She turned a critical eye on her most recent canvas. It was a portrayal of the view from the back of the house, itself an intriguing jumble of wooden verandah and steeply sloping roof. A portrayal that was wilder, somehow than the reality. There was the glow of the marsh, its feathery reedy breathing skin. In the foreground barbed wire, a fence unravelling, stakes askew, with a single bird, a stonechat, on a high bramble tangle, half dancing in the wind, battling to keep its perch. A glimpse, that's all, with air and light the protagonists, the background half blurry with heat.

Yesterday evening she'd stood on the verandah savouring the

view. Everything was perfectly still. She'd taken a deep breath and had drunk in the landscape, just as she caught sight of a kestrel's golden hovering, its sudden plunge.

'*The trouble with you is you don't accept the world as it is* ....' Those had been Stephen's words some months back when they were still together, just about. Yet again she'd challenged him, this time about his relationship with their next door neighbour, an attractive divorcee. Joy just couldn't believe he'd have the sheer nerve to carry on with someone right on their very doorstep, but nerve, and downright cheek were attributes Our Hero had in plenty. He expected Joy to accept him for the man he was, to accept the reality of his philandering nature and she just couldn't. There were so many other things she couldn't accept either; the fact so much of life involved struggle and pain. From injured blackbirds, to plunging kestrels — there was so much of it and Joy's sensitivity was such that she found it all hard to bear. She so often felt a disproportionate vulnerability, a kind of terror.

It was this vision of the world that made her, that above all made her paint.

* * * *

When Abbie arrived Joy took out a couple of kitchen chairs and put them on the verandah so they could sit out. Anne and Sally were already out there on the hammock-style swing.

'This could be the deep South,' Abbie said laughing. 'All we need are our mint juleps.'

'Or our southern comforts,' said Joy.

It was a dry dusty summer that made the days languid and slow. They lounged away the morning dreamily, Joy telling Abbie not long after she arrived that Stephen would be making an appearance later.

'How are things between you now?' Abbie asked.

Joy shrugged her shoulders. 'I don't know,' she said. 'I don't, really. The very thought of Our Hero and his winning ways gets me in a flat spin. I suppose I have to admit that I miss him a lot, but I can't see us ever getting back together again. Besides, I like my independence here. This place suits me.' Abbie was aware that Joy was being brave about her present circumstances. She could feel an underlying tension and sadness behind her words.

It was then Stephen arrived.

Joy wasn't surprised to see his face light up as soon as he saw Abbie, and sure enough, the legendary charm was immediately in evidence.

'Why don't we go for a walk on the beach,' he suggested. 'There's one thing I can't understand — people who live by the sea just take it for granted and hardly ever even look at it.'

'I look at it plenty,' said Joy. 'I keep trying to paint it effectively but it doesn't work out, I don't know why.'

Stephen led the way as if he was on an expedition. Abbie was getting his full attention and Anne and Joy exchanged long looks with each other, as it to say, m'mm, we might have guessed. Joy and her elder daughter often exchanged notes on Stephen's activities. 'He's just a born flirt,' Anne told her mother. 'He can't help it,' and again Joy found herself wondering whether she should have learned to ignore his philandering. She reckoned other women might be able to. She thought of all those mediaeval queens who had to tolerate the presence of their husband's mistresses at court. There was so much about Stephen that was lovable, that was fun. She had lost a great deal in saying enough was enough. Pride was her bastion now.

They walked along the sea wall for a while and then crossed the slithery bank of pebbles to get down to the sand. The tide was going out leaving a damp glinting surface behind the retreating waves.

'Look,' said Sally suddenly. 'What are all those?' She was pointing right down the beach to the far fringe of the bay near the lifeboat station. There were lots of small objects near the waterline, dozens of strange things which seemed to have been left behind by the tide.

'Let's go and see what they are,' said Sally immediately, and in no time she and Anne were running along the sand towards the mystery.

'Perhaps they're baby jellyfish,' said Anne. 'There's loads and loads of them.'

When the three adults reached the girls they agreed that these puzzling stranded creatures were most likely to be baby jellyfish though no one present had ever seen anything remotely resembling them before. They were at most three inches long and bright blue with what for all the world looked like sails on their backs, made of nature's own variant on a theme in some sort of fluted plastic or polythene.

'Don't touch them,' Joy warned. 'They might sting.'

'Can we take some of them home with us,' said Sally. 'I could take them to school and see if Mr Edwards Biology knows what they are.'

'You'll have to carry them home in something,' Stephen said. He looked at the sea's odd harvest at his feet. 'Perhaps you could bring the washing up bowl or something.'

Joy pulled a face at the thought of these creatures in her washing up bowl but she wasn't seriously opposed to the idea. The girls both ran off, back to the house, leaving Our Hero and the two women on the shore, standing on the smooth sand where the jellyfish lay, as if they were guarding them.

After they got back with their trophies Stephen said he'd take them all out to tea somewhere. Joy, who would have much preferred him to just take the girls, so she and Abbie could have a chat on their own and catch up with their news, resisted at first but no, Our Hero was adamant. It would be his treat. He found what had once been farm outbuildings but were now a little restaurant and craft centre. He bought the girls Celtic pendants, one of violet stones, the other dark green and moody, and would have, with any encouragement, bought Joy an angora blanket and Abbie a tablecloth. He was at his boisterous best, generous, expansive. Joy watched as he set out to win Abbie over with his charm. Her feelings were muddled. Reluctant love mixed with something that was never hate, but skimmed quite close to it. When he finally went, half an hour or so after bringing them home, the house was unnaturally quiet, was colourless.

There was quite a commotion in the kitchen early the next morning. The girls were the first to get up, and the first thing they did was inspect the jellyfish.

'Aw mum,' Sally yelled. 'Just look at this.'

Joy came to see. The little bright blue strangers in the washing up bowl were no more. All that was left was a pulpy bluish-green mess that smelled to high heaven.

'Oh, aren't we stupid,' Joy remonstrated. 'I know now what we should have done. We should have left them in salt water. They'd have had a chance then.'

Abbie, too, was furious with herself for not thinking.

'We'll never know what they were now,' said Anne.

Joy got hold of the bowl. 'I'm going to flush what's left of them down the loo,' she said determinedly.

Abbie saw her friend's face streaked with tears, and thought of how she'd had to toughen up as a young doctor on the ward for the first time. Joy would never have been able to adapt, to learn the hard, necessary lessons of detachment. She thought of Stephen's easy superficial charm, of Joy's susceptibility. She went to the window and looked out at the great bowl of the sky surging with clouds, the earth itself marked with the racing clouds' shadows.

The Boy at Pydew

There were three girls on the bridge, sitting there on the parapet of sunny stone and it was out of the green blur of the lane and down from the hill came Monkey, his pale lurcher ambling by his side, and little Billy Talbot trying to keep up behind him. They had shotguns over their shoulders.

'D'you want a bunny?' Monkey shouted at them, nudging Billy sharply in the ribs as they passed.

'No. No we don't. You're cruel, you. Clear off.'

That was Marged. Adamant.

Vinnie could still see it all, even the clothes they were wearing, Marged in that black skinny rib despite the heat, Denise with her bell-bottoms, literally bell-bottoms, the strip of chiming silver tinkling as she unwrapped her legs from under her. As the boys disappeared, swaggering, turning in to Jac y Felin's in a minute, no doubt, to compare notes with their guide and mentor, they were laughing to themselves, making slurped kissing noises and generally being the idiots they were.

There were rabbits alright, two of them each, hanging down their backs, in Monkey's case from some sort of leather strap with hooks, but another slimmer creature was hanging there too. Different, grey golden this one, seemingly, in the mottling sunlight that fell through the sycamores. Long legs dangling, a lithe, waltzing shape, going with the swing, the bump on his back.

And Marged was up like a shot and after them.

'You've killed a hare,' she screamed at them. 'They're rare, hares.'

'Well, what d'you know, Billy. We've got a rare hare here,' Monkey said laughing, showing all the too many teeth in his mouth, and there was Billy's round face glistening up at him. Sickening. Rising to the occasion Monkey had to put on a posh huntin' and shootin' voice and said it again, just in case anyone had missed it first time round. 'How about that? We've got a rare hare here.'

Billy, of course, said nothing. He never did. He just adored.

They were gone then, Vinnie looking sideways at Marged as she glowered, face red, eyes blinded, brimming.

'My mother says jugged hare is delicious,' Denise cut in, her voice as sharp and deceptively sweet as those daft bells of hers. 'Tender flesh, she says. Melts in the mouth.'

'Why don't you go after them, then? Get yourself some for your supper?' said Marged. 'Give them one of those cute little smiles of yours. I'm sure Monkey'd oblige.'

'Oh, he would. He would. But I don't want any, thanks all the same. My mother says people used to eat a lot of hare in the war, actually.'

'Perhaps that's why they're rare then,' Vinnie added. It was only a harmless comment, addressed half to herself. There was something strangely human, somehow, about the way that hare'd been hanging. It made you feel peculiar. Sort of vulnerable and threatened, more so than the sight of the rabbits.

But this was the last straw for Marged. She was off, the rage in her like a forcefield, tangible, so even the cloud of midges by the water dispersed before her. First of all she went storming off in the direction the lads had taken, then, thinking better of that, she turned back up the lane the way they'd come, passing the two on the bridge without so much as a glance in their direction.

Vinnie was sorry she'd said anything about the hare with Marged in such a fly off the handle mood. She was on Marged's side, after all. She always was, but Denise had such a sly way with her, and Marged always rose to her bait. Best leave her to it in this sort of state. She wouldn't go far on her own, would she? There was nothing up there but the track to Esgair Wen and the forestry. And none of them, not even Marged, could stand the creepiness, the quiet of those straight lines of trees.

Upset as she was about Marged, and that painful picture of the hare in her mind that she just couldn't get rid of, and no matter how sick she was of Denise's prattle, she was too hot, too lazy to move, unable to, stuck, it felt, to the hot stone of the bridge, the small murmur of insects and water. They waited for Marged. Ages. But she didn't come back.

'We'd better go,' Denise said. 'We can't hang about here for ever.'

'You go if you like. I'm staying.'

And a few minutes after the bells had trembled out of earshot Marged was back, but not sulky as you'd expect. 'I've seen that boy at Pydew,' she said, eager and different, and really pretty, like she was sometimes when Denise wasn't there.

Vinnie would normally have said so what? Hadn't she been the first to see him, after all, walking down the steep field by Jac y Felin's, with the swathes of bracken, the mill race clogged with debris, the smudge of deeper green all around where it was swampy. And with a gold cat round his neck. Half wild they said it was, but he'd trained it so it ran to him like a dog.

'Are you sure it isn't a dog?' Denise had asked quietly, sitting with the other two in the kitchen at Marged's while they watched her drying her new Coral Glimmer nail varnish with Marged's hair drier. Her slim pale fingers were arranged on the tablecloth like ornaments.

'Of course it's a cat. I'm not stupid,' Vinnie had said, angry at Denise's sheer poise, her total belief in her own superiority, that way she had of pouring cold water on anything either of the other two ever said. Which was why, now, confronted with Marged's hectic brightness, she simply listened, telling her she was sorry about the hare too, that she understood. That they were friends. The best.

* * * *

So much had changed at Pydew.

Twenty years earlier the boy with the feral cat had arrived and transformed the place. Before he came Pydew had worn an air of dilapidation, even despair. Stefan's uncle Bryn had let the place go to the dogs.

There was some sympathy for him. It wasn't as if he were naturally shiftless. When his wife and new born daughter both died years back on a hot August night it was as if the world had gone dark for Bryn. 'I haven't done much with the place since the wife went,' he'd say apologetically over The Red Lion's best draught bitter. When his sister appeared one day in a huge American car with a man in a cowboy hat, a Country and Western singer she'd met in a club in Cardiff, by all accounts, and literally dumped her son on him, how the stories circulated. Mind you Cassie'd always been, well, a handful, shall we say. Stefan certainly acquired a disreputable glamour to his name. It could have been Welsh but was actually Polish after his father, a mythic character, as impermanent as the rest.

The boy with the gold cat which draped itself round his shoulders captured the imagination of the village. He was different, even exotic. Stories grew about him, a veritable aura developed. Apparently he tamed the birds, especially a pair of goldfinches folk had seen flying along the hedges to be near him as he walked down the lane. Denise had scoffed. 'Anyone would think he was our very own St Francis', she said, having her own reasons for disparaging him.

Stefan certainly had a wonderful way with animals of all kinds. That summer he arrived, a dog, Mrs Pendleton's Great

Dane, no less, had fallen in a limepit on the site where they were building new bungalows by the church. The dog was crazed with the burning of the lime in its eyes but somehow Stefan had managed to calm it when no one else dared get near, had gently and carefully bathed those burning eyes in water and saved the dog's sight.

If Stefan was something of a miracle worker his greatest achievement was the amazing change he brought about at Pydew itself, and primarily with Bryn. No one knew how Bryn survived to tell the truth, before Stefan came. How did he manage? Did he have some money invested somewhere? All he ever did was let his fields for grazing. More prosperous farmers would use Bryn's green acres to fatten their own black calves.

Anyway, with Stefan's arrival things started to happen at Pydew, but it wasn't as if the boy did all the work himself. No, it was more that his industry and cheerfulness acted as a catalyst, changing Bryn, so that the idle days dried up and he took to working about the place the way he'd done before, buying calves of his own this time, a few sheep. He grew potatoes, a splendid crop, putting up a sign at the roadside which drew the buyers in. Then he bought hens and sold free range eggs. Meanwhile Stefan had started on transforming the look of the place, painting and decorating, seeing to it that fences were repaired, gates were mended.

On the day Marged stormed off on her own, the day of the hare, she saw the boy at Pydew for the first time. She was not the only one to have her eye on him. Once school started again Denise made a bee-line for him, but somehow her Sea Witch blonde-in-a-bottle hair and her painted fingernails had no effect. It wasn't as if he had no interest in girls either, it was just that he was so constantly busy he didn't have time. This active manliness was part of his appeal. Somehow he wasn't like the other boys. He'd grown up. He was self-contained, self-reliant. He'd had to be with a mother like Cassie and a succession of shortlived and distinctly dubious father figures.

Stefan had learned two valuable lessons very early in life. The first was not to care what other people thought, the second was to amuse and entertain himself. He didn't need to cover his natural shyness with bravado and rudeness. There was a stillness, a completeness about him.

It was paradoxical. The more self-sufficient Stefan became the more he attracted the admiration of the girls in the village. He seemed not to need people the way others did, but somehow his quiet, reticent manner gave other people confidence, made them quite simply feel good about themselves. This was what eventually happened, long after they'd both left school, when Stefan took an interest in Vinnie. She blossomed visibly. It was something of a whirlwind romance on the outside, but this is only what it appeared to be. Vinnie had carried a torch for Stefan for a long time, and he'd noticed her too, right from the start.

Vinnie continued with her job as a doctor's receptionist after their marriage, until the children came along. Stefan worked for the forestry. It might have been difficult having Bryn around but he wisely gave the young couple plenty of space, and it was Vinnie who eventually nursed Bryn through his last illness, keeping him at home till the very end, despite the fact that by then she and Stefan had three children. Vinnie's father had died while she was still at school and Bryn had replaced him in her affections. Somehow life at Pydew, even in the saddest times, was good, was wholesome and sure. This is what Marged often said. 'Everyone pulls together here. It's wonderful. The atmosphere's like nowhere else I know.'

Marged had never married. She taught History in the local High School and was in many ways still the earnest, idealistic creature she'd been in her teens. Vinnie knew in some subtle way that Marged was at least half in love with Stefan, always had been. It never worried her. She was sure of Stefan's steadfastness as much as Marged's loyalty, but knowing what she knew gave the women's relationship an extra dimension. They'd never stopped being friends, both of them being relieved and pleased when Denise left the village years earlier.

What was it about her that blighted everything? Neither admitted it in so many words but both Marged and Vinnie had been frightened of Denise, her talent for manipulation and division, her spiteful tongue. Just occasionally she came back to the village to see her mother but that had stopped now, ever since her mother'd been left a considerable sum of money and a house in Builth Wells, moving away some years before. There was no reason for Denise to visit the village anymore. No one had seen her for years and no one was sorry.

They'd virtually forgotten her existence.

* * * *

'They've got to be English, whoever they are,' said Stefan. 'They've got more money than sense.'

He was talking about the renovation job they were doing at Y Felin. It had taken a long time to get the run-down Pydew back on its feet but this was a different matter altogether, especially since it was only a few months back since Jac y Felin's death. In no time at all, it seemed, the old place was sold and a thoroughgoing refurbishing was well under way.

Vinnie reckoned middle age must be fast approaching since lately she'd developed a pronounced resistance to change. She liked things to stay the same. It was reassuring. Jac had been a fixture in the village and it seemed he'd always be standing there at his gate, waiting for the likes of Monkey and Billy Talbot to come by. Mind you, things hadn't turned out the way you'd imagine as far as they were concerned. Who'd ever have guessed that Monkey would get the job of school caretaker, becoming almost respectable in the process, or that Billy Talbot would join the army? You could never tell.

Jac was old admittedly, but his death was still sudden, unexpected. He'd been the last of the village characters, seemingly ancient and unchangeable even when Vinnie and Marged were schoolgirls. Vinnie remembered being sent on an errand there when Jac had recently come home from hospital after a gall bladder operation. She'd taken him one of her mother's special lemon cakes. Never before had she made her way through the dank, ivy-bangled trees to Y Felin on her own. She'd never forget its unique green gloom, the sound of water dripping *plick plick* somewhere out of sight. The building hadn't been used as a working mill since the First World War, but the water wheel was still there, if rotten, with hart's tongue ferns and mosses growing on the wall around it. Inside everything was covered with a film of dust, the air smelled heavily of cats, and on the dresser, proud with a collection of Delft blue dinner plates, all crazed with minute lines like ancient faces, there were dozens of brown envelopes representing years and years of bills, paid on the nail with fierce old chapel pride and stubbornness, the receipts kept like medals.

Now those dank trees had been felled, the mill house was shown in its entirety as potentially a very handsome building indeed. The old stone was sandblasted revealing an attractive grey-yellow like Cotswold limestone, the yard to the front painstakingly cobbled with seashore pebbles in the traditional style. A new mill wheel replaced the old one, though this was purely for decorative purposes, and the swampy field where the mill race had once run was expertly drained and replaced by a sparkling new millpond. An old village landmark appeared in a totally fresh light as the luxurious and very fashionable home of strangers.

Strangers? Well, not quite.

* * * *

Vinnie picked up the envelope. It was a Saturday. Stefan and the children were having a bit of a lie in, but she'd heard the postman, and went downstairs to see what had been delivered. Now, holding an unexpected invitation in her hand, she opened the door and looked outside.

From Pydew she could see right across the narrow valley, the dip where the river ran, and the spot where on sunny days long ago three girls would often be found sitting, idling, on a grey stone bridge. The sycamores through which the light had fallen, mottling the coat of the slaughtered hare that day, were still there, handsome trees secure in their maturity. These broke the view across to Y Felin, which was just out of sight, denuded of its old decaying trees now. Vinnie could see the house in her mind's eye, the suddenly foreign place it was.

Never, not even for a moment, had she thought Denise was at the back of it, yet a certain flamboyance and speed in the execution might have betrayed her, if Vinnie'd been given a clue that Denise was even the least bit interested in reclaiming her roots. Vinnie looked again at her invitation to the house warming, the sprawling signature ... Denise and Reg. Reg had a lot of money, whoever he was. Something plunged and plummeted in her stomach. Marged, Vinnie was sure, would also have received an invitation. It was just then the telephone rang.

'Come round soon as you can and we'll talk about it,' said Vinnie. At this moment the tousled head of Sion, her nine year old eldest, appeared round the kitchen door. 'Aren't there any Coco Pops left, mum?' he asked.

'Have some Weetabix instead,' said Vinnie. 'I'll get some

next time I do a big shop. Alright? Aunty Marged's coming round for a chat in a minute. There's something we want to talk about.'

* * * *

It was Stefan who clarified the situation for them. it was so obvious, so simple and yet it had seemed to Vinnie and Marged that they were being drawn back helplessly into Denise's web. 'You don't have to go, do you?' he said. 'You can always say thanks but no thanks. She can't make you do anything you don't want to do.'

The truth hit them like a revelation. Denise might be around again, wanting to get back into their lives, but they didn't have to let her have her own way, did they? There was no doubt she'd want to play her old power games again, as well as show off her new home which would undoubtedly be more sumptuous than anything for miles around. Owning Y Felin would have novelty value for her, a second home in the country to retreat to. Life in the village would be too quiet in the long run, though, Stefan thought, especially if Denise's former victims refused to play ball. Where was the challenge then? What would be the point of it? Suddenly Marged's honesty owned up to something that was equally true for her friend.

'I feel so stupid when I admit that I'm actually scared of her,' she said.

'So do I,' Vinnie still fingered the invitation as if it might blow up in her hands. 'Even now it's hard to say exactly what it was about her that got to me all the time. I don't know what it was to tell the truth.'

Then she looked across the table at Stefan. He was the opposite of Denise. He gave her strength where Denise had only weakened her; he made her feel secure where Denise had undermined. I'm so lucky to have him, to have all this, Vinnie thought. Eluned was scraping loudly at her cereal bowl, Sion groping for his wellies in the cupboard under the sink. Her youngest, little Stefan, sat beside Marged, watching intently as she drew for him a whole family of cartoon cats with his favourite thick felt pen.

The Gingerbread House

'It all seems so, well, feudal. Quaint.'

'Does it?'

I'd never thought of it in those terms. The first eight years of my life had been an island out of time, yes, I'd felt that. But the sheer oddity of it all in terms of other people's experience just hadn't occurred to me. And ending as those eight years did, with such drama, such pain and mystery, it seemed as if someone had pulled the curtains down on a bright stage. Afterwards nothing could be the same.

John pulled the car up on the other side of the road.

'D'you want to get out? Have a proper look round?'

The lodge looked the same, the gingerbread house of my childhood. They say when you go back to a childhood haunt it always seems to have shrunk. This hadn't changed at all. There were the same ecclesiastical style windows, with the stained glass, the fretwork frieze around the gables. There was the crest in plaster on the wall above the front door, its plaited porch. The brandycurl chimneys were as they'd always been, twisty and enchanting, and the drive up to the Captain's house remained its inviting self. Two huge ilex trees stood breathlessly waiting, commanding the scene as they always did. Noble trees, shapes that have stayed in my mind, standing a little apart from us, so distinctly themselves, bearing around them their own weather. It was always a perfected scene, a freeze-frame that symbolized a season. There must have been grey drab days but I don't remember them. I see only the richness of summer, feel again the smoky nearness of autumn, the clarity of white winters.

I didn't live at the lodge. It might never have seemed so

magical if I had. I lived in one of the identical red-brick Reservoir Houses we'd left behind us as we first drove in to the valley, taking the left hand turn at the junction. The road on the right climbed steeply up into a bareness inhabited only by sheep. The lake itself was up there. The Reservoir Houses struck me today as ugly but surprisingly substantial. They'd been built two years before my birth, to replace two drowned small-holdings and one half-empty terrace. Drowned too were the old quarry workings, defunct since my grandfather's day. How had the people taken it as inevitable, my father one of them? How had they accepted it so passively? It could never happen now. That, at least, signified change, invisible maybe, in this slumbering place, but real, for all that. I saw what John meant about feudalism.

My father had always worked for the Captain, his father too, before him. They were tied to him, his family, in a state of comfortable dependence. Things would have stayed exactly the same if it had not been for what happened that day, when Yann came back without warning. Three violent deaths brought about a violent change in my father. He suddenly started to think for himself, to act, rather than simply be acted upon. Admittedly there was no work for him here now, not afterwards, but the speed with which he organised our move away, and away for good, was startling to say the least.

I think somehow he was afraid for us, his wife and daughter, felt that the influence of the rebel Ennis, even in death, was all pervasive. We had to be taken away from this place and within three months we'd left the valley behind us for ever. We never talked about our life there. He wouldn't let us, wanting to erase it all. I'm sure this great need of his, for finality, for silence, only made me feel more and more that I'd been banished from paradise.

We left just before Christmas, spent that festival in blankness, disorientated, living out of boxes in our bleak new home. I remember my first day in the new school, writing the date importantly in my exercise books, the special year that marked the new decade: 1960. It seems to me now, fanciful though I acknowledge it to be, that I'd already lived through the pattern of the decade that lay ahead, experienced all its elations and traumas, the dream that became a nightmare. And I see Ennis and Yann, both of them never to see the sixties, as archetypes, somehow, of that unforgettable time. In them were the aspirations, the experiments, the alternatives, tasted and tried and in due course found wanting; grown decadent, finally, all ending in a bloodbath, in violent death. But of course this is not how I thought at the time, not how I saw it then. I was not yet nine years old. I'm not sure that I understood what had happened till years later, Not fully, in fact, till today, if what my mother told me was true. As far as I could see she had no reason to lie to me.

There had been Ennis, lively summery Ennis with her laughter, her freckles and funny clothes, especially that floppy sombrero. I remember her wearing this, sitting in bright sun in the garden of the lodge, shelling peas. My mother was captivated by Ennis. So was I. She kept goats. She cooked brown rice. I don't suppose she did actually wear either beads or sandals, but my memory has her dressed like that, in flimsy long colourful things. She was a hippie, a free spirit, before such things were thought of. Ahead of her time.

And Yann, another exotic, the merchant seaman, the traveller to foreign parts, his strange guttural English. He brought things back from his voyagings, wonderful things, the like of which the valley had never seen, a mah yong set, a hookah, the most exquisite silks. He turned the globe for me, pointing to the places he'd just visited. Rio de Janeiro. Singapore. He told me stories, held me agog with his worlds of zombies and voodoo.

No one I'd ever seen looked like Yann. He wore an earring when no man wore an earring, ever. He looked like a pirate, emanating energy. I could imagine him with a patch over one eye, a knife between his teeth, a cutlass ....

Once he called me to him as I sat in their cool leaf-green kitchen, drinking the frothy goat milk I did not like but always accepted so as not to disappoint Ennis. (How earnest I was, how eager to please. I know now, more than twenty years later, that Ennis would have laughed aloud to think I drank something I did not like simply to please her.) 'Here,' he said. 'For you, Delyth. (How odd my name sounded the way he said it!) I buy this for you.'

And he handed me a flurry of crackling-alive blue tissue paper, swathes of it. Inside there was a fan, with dragons humming patchouli.

* * * *

I am here again, back again in the valley of the idyll. This is the gingerbread house, here, in front of me, and this is the fairy tale place where I was as happy as if I lived in a dream.

My father was the Captain's right hand man. He was gardener, painter and decorator, odd job man, and chauffeur, too on occasion, but they were also friends. Apparently accepting his role in life without question, he was nonetheless never over-deferential. In fact the Captain, in a boyish way, would often defer to his experience. My father was a good mechanic. Any problem with a tractor or bailer or whatever up at the Home Farm and my father would be there, patient and unhurried, always thorough, always more than competent. When we moved he soon found work in the town. Always he'd had this way with engines, made them sing under his hands, and soon customers at the garage were asking for him by name.

At last he was being paid proper money, too, for the first time in his life.

But in many ways he was a changed man, and not for the better. He was hard on us, especially my mother. I think now that he believed Ennis' influence had changed her from the quiet chapel girl he'd married into a potential, well, I don't know. A scarlet woman, I suppose. It was ridiculous. My mother was still the biddable creature she'd always been, more so. The shootings, understandably, had frightened her, shaken her. She was lost in this new place, still, and always, the country girl at heart. Sometimes she seemed to have become almost simple, and how cruelly my father would lash her with his tongue if she was clumsy in serving his meal, or failed to sew a button on his shirt. I never heard them have an ordinary, affectionate conversation. Not any more. Certainly Ennis had fascinated my mother, had drawn her, as the flame draws the moth. I think, too, the other, so much more vital woman, had been amused by this devotion. But my father failed to understand that for my mother, Ennis, and Yann, too, were scarcely real people. Their behaviour, their attitudes were in no way to be emulated. She treated them more as film stars, that had somehow miraculously brought unaccustomed glamour into her humdrum life. They were no mere human flesh and blood.

And as for the Captain .... My mother was quite unable to come to terms with it. Her friendship with Ennis, too, gone, so abruptly, so horribly. She thought of Ennis and she thought of Yann. It couldn't be true. We could none of us believe they were dead. That Yann had returned, early and unexpectedly, found the Captain and Ennis together, shot them both, then turned the gun on himself, to die in hospital two days later. Things like this didn't happen in our world. In the days that followed I heard snippets here, snippets there, trying to tie it all together, to make sense of it. I remember I'd heard someone say that Yann had found the Captain in Ennis' bed, and that puzzled me. What could he have been doing there? I'd seen the sheer size of the Captain's house, having walked along the drive there many times after school to meet my father. The Captain had dozens of bedrooms and surely dozens of beds of his own. As I was forbidden to speak of our life in the valley once we'd moved away, it was a thoroughly bewildered and frightened child who tried to put a shape, a meaning on what had happened.

'This is a weird place,' John said. We'd left the car and were walking in the still October evening away from the lodge and up to a slight rise on the right where beech trees stood golden and radiant. 'There's such a static atmosphere,' he went on. 'It's like a film set.' For me time had stopped abruptly in the valley when we left. I was glad he felt it too.

When the reservoir was completed, and the shiny new Reservoir Houses built, the new lake needed a name. The Captain suggested Llyn Hud, the lake of enchantment, a choice that tells us at least as much about the captain himself as the nature of the land that had been in his family for generations. Thoroughly English in his speech and in his manner (his education had seen to that) he retained romantic Celtic leanings in plenty. Money seemed to escape him, running away from him like water. Ventures galore ended in failure, the mushroom farm, the deer park. He was always ready with yet another idea, in that, at least irrepressible, languidly handsome, joking and kindly, and often more than a little the worse for drink. He would carry a silver hip flask concealed in a jacket pocket. Whenever he came round to see my father, and they stood chatting in the garden, my mother coming out with the tea, (and suddenly I'm there again, of a summer evening, the scent of bean flowers heavy on the air) he'd add a nip from that quick, glinting flask and offer it, half-surreptitiously. My father always refused.

As I think back to that old life I try to see the captain's face, to visualise it. I can't. Yann and Ennis are etched so clearly, but my memory of him is only that of a presence and a voice; the presence gentle, literally self-effacing, the voice with its well-bred purr, its slightly clipped intonation. He was a tall man, but there's only a hollow, an absence where he stands.

'Are you ready to go up to the lake now?' John asked me. I nodded. We'd planned an itinerary since leaving our home in Carlisle yesterday, our two children with John's parents. This morning, and how strange it sounds to say this, we'd been guests at my mother's wedding. No one could have been more surprised to receive the invitation than I'd been, a couple of months earlier. My father had been dead for years, my mother continuing to live in the same house, her life largely going on as it had always done, without incident, predictable in its patterns. But a couple of years ago, at Christmas, she'd written to say she'd started to attend an evangelical church. John had been contemptuous. 'So she's joined the happy-clappy brigade, has she', he snorted. He disliked my mother. As the story of my childhood had been revealed to him, bit by bit, he increasingly came to despise my parents, the misery they'd inflicted upon themselves, and, above all, on me.

In John, for the first time ever, I had a true ally, someone at last who took my part. After my father's death I thought my mother and I might grow closer but it didn't happen, and when John was offered promotion away I was glad to leave. When our own children were born my mother sent little presents but showed no interest in coming to see them. Until this morning, we'd not seen each other for seven years, and it has to be said that John was a reluctant guest. I told him I'd go on my own if he didn't want to come with me, that despite our differences I wanted to wish my mother well. Curiosity played its part too. I wanted to see what this step-father of mine was like. He was the minister at the church, no less, a Pastor Edwin Dawkes, a widower with twin teenage daughters. I was thoroughly intrigued.

John and I stayed overnight in a small hotel by the river. It was he who suggested that, after the wedding in the morning, we'd go and take a look at the valley he'd heard so much about. Naturally, since as a child I was never even allowed to talk about the place, I'd certainly never been there again, and eventually, as the years went by, I lost all interest in returning. The idea of going there with John, though, appealed more and more. Suddenly, I felt I wanted so much to show him our old home and the gingerbread house itself. I wanted to see if the valley really was as beautiful as I remembered, and if it was still haunted by the tragedy that took place there so long ago. There was also something I'd never actually mentioned to John, a secret childhood ritual I'd carried out in my imagination again and again. I wanted to re-enact this in reality, if it seemed appropriate and right to do it.

But something happened at the wedding that made me realise, even at this late stage, how little I knew about my parents after all, how totally I'd failed to understand my father's hostile attitude towards us.

The service itself was simple and pleasing. John was relieved to find it wasn't 'happy-clappy' at all, and I was relieved for him, knowing how embarrassing he found extravagant outbursts of piety. My mother actually looked younger than I remembered her. Seven years ago she'd been extremely thin and drawn. Now her hairstyle was softer, the harsh lines around her mouth had disappeared, and the gain in weight had improved her appearance no end. She was positively serene in a pale green knitted suit and a large-brimmed dark green hat.

The man responsible for this extraordinary change had a frank open face and a firm handshake. Even John had to admit

Pastor Edwin Dawkes was reassuringly normal. When I met my new step-sisters, however, I have to own up to being briefly jealous. My mother was so relaxed and at ease with these blonde, stolid girls that I felt distinctly left out, resentful, too, that, since there was obviously affection in plenty to be bestowed on these strangers, she'd never so much as asked to see her own grandchildren. Perhaps things would be different now though, I told myself. It was as if my mother had been asleep for years, listless, half-alive only. Now she seemed to have been restored to a former self.

The reception was held in the church hall, and there were about sixty guests. While people helped themselves from a generous buffet and milled around informally, my mother came across to talk to me, John discreetly moving away to leave us together.

'Del,' she said, and it was so long since I'd heard that diminutive, my sense of distance, of reserve, was gone at once. 'I've tried time and time again to write to you, but I couldn't find the words for what I wanted to say.'

'What is it, mum?' I said, grabbing the hand she held uncertainly towards me.

'I'm just so sorry,' she said, 'so sorry for everything that happened.'

'It wasn't your fault,' I said, but she wouldn't let me go on.

'The reason your father,' she paused, 'the reason there was always such tension at home, was my fault really. You don't know the half, Del.'

'What don't I know?'

'I never forgave him, you see.' She gulped. 'It wasn't just the Captain, your father loved Ennis, too. Yes, they were lovers. You never guessed that, did you? With the shock of their deaths, and the Captain's, he told me all about it, confessing in tears, and I pushed him away. He was full of guilt, and the feeling that Yann should have shot him too. That never left him. It was a terrible stalemate, the very worst kind of environment for a child to grow up in. Lately, thanks to Edwin, I feel I've come alive emotionally again. I hope, Del, it's not too late, that I can make amends.'

'Everything's alright, mum,' I said. 'I've come through it, haven't I? And I've got John, and the boys. I'm really very lucky.'

She squeezed my hand and fought back tears. 'I'll see you again before you go,' she said.

I went back to John, picking at a laden plate, trying to come to terms with what I'd heard, trying to see my father as Ennis's lover, failing frankly, but aware, deep down, that what my mother had told me was true. I thought of Ennis herself. Perhaps for the first time my awe and admiration for her wavered. When all I remembered of my contact with her was so warm, so positive, how could she have been an agent of such destruction? Questions buzzed through my mind like bees. Had my father known about the Captain and Ennis beforehand? Had there been others? Our sleepy, peaceful valley had contained such passion, such extremity, it still felt unreal. I suddenly felt sorry for my father. With a woman like Ennis he must have been out of his depth. And he'd always been so involved with the Captain too — for him to survive and the Captain to die .... I saw Ennis so clearly, myself beside her, picking raspberries in the garden, her large freckled hands lifting the green nets that kept the birds away. I saw the fruit fall into a chipped enamel bowl, heard her low musical voice, her words, inconsequential maybe, but so welcoming.

John and I went back to the car, setting off this time in the direction of the steep road to the reservoir. Here I was astonished to find things were not at all as I remembered them, that the sad little ritual I'd enacted every night in my mind before going to sleep had nothing to do with this featureless mountain cleft, this dark water. Every night I'd envisaged a gentle valley, clasped between hills, their lower slopes clothed with deciduous forest. The lake had, on one side, little bays and inlets, pebbly shores and alder trees with delicate cones and catkins. I saw myself walking quietly by the water's edge, dressed in a hooded cloak something like Red Riding Hood's, but of a dark material. I was carrying something blue in my hands, held out in front of me, solemnly. When I came to the largest of the alder trees I set my bundle down (it was the dragon fan Yann had given me, still wrapped in its thin tissue) and started to dig with a trowel I had in my pocket. Mouthing a whole sequence of prayers and magical charms (I was hedging my bets!) I buried it carefully, and then walked away feeling so much happier, soothed and at peace. I'd realised for a long time that this bedtime ritual had been my attempt to get rid of the past, and that constantly repeating it proved only that the past could not be so easily disposed of.

In all the intervening years the one thing I hadn't told John was how crucially significant the ritual had become, and that I'd brought the fan with me on this pilgrimage, intending to bury it once and for all, and for real.

But the choppy gunmetal water and the stark shore were a shock to me. The difference between the scene in my mind and this unrelieved bleakness underlined all the other mistakes I'd made, those false interpretations. My father had not been harsh with us because he saw us as potentially evil. His surliness, his sullen detachment were due to his own feelings of unworthiness. I saw how much my parents had been the products of their narrow upbringing, how guilt and anger had warped their lives.

And I began to see how inappropriate, now, were the images I'd superimposed on my childhood past. The gingerbread house was not a house in a fairy tale at all, but the brick and mortar dwelling of someone who was neither a witch nor a fairy creature, merely an attractive woman with a strong sexual appetite and a scanty conscience. Yann was no longer the romantic hero either. He seemed to shrink in stature, while the Captain, I saw for the first time, was essentially a pathetic figure. I had been a little girl exposed to the destructive effects of adult emotions I could not hope to even begin to understand.

'I never showed you the fan, John, did I? The one Yann gave me?'

'No,' he said, turning towards me as I produced it from the crinkly blue sheets in my bag. That symbol of feminine coquetry was no exquisite piece of carving but a cheap flimsy object, though as I unwrapped it the scent of patchouli was still surprisingly strong. Slowly I opened the fan and closed it again.

'I don't know why I've kept this all these years,' I said. 'I seemed to need to hold on to it.'

'You don't now, do you?'

'There'll be the autumn fair at the school soon,' I told him. 'I'll send it along with those old paperbacks we said we'd clear out.' I looked up at him and smiled.

A Wildness of Starlings

Sometimes specific memories acquire a significance way beyond any obvious single meaning, become symbolic, somehow, of a whole period in one's life, its special tone and colour, its *leitmotif.*

There was one image, one memory of Anne's that did just this. It was winter. She was standing with Jay on the sloping bank that marked the drop down to the beach road, the promenade which followed the curve of the bay, and which right now was closed off to all traffic. It was the aftermath of the storm, but the weather was still wild. Rocks and pebbles had been flung onto the road by waves like mountains. They were now like hills, slithery salty inundations that swept the promenade with regular grey falls, solid walls of water.

It was a week or two after Christmas, only tea-time, but already nearly dark. There was still a pocket of lurid light in the sky though, just above the pier. There they were, hand in hand, Anne and Jay on the bank with the spindly pines behind them, the pier in front of them. And there was the extraordinary baroque pier theatre with its gilded onion domes, that were somehow forlorn and tawdry as well as exotic. Anne loved that theatre. It was so over the top, so tasteless. It belonged to another age, standing in squat bulbous homage to the Brighton pavilion. It had never quite worked. Its proportions were wrong. It was vulgar and it was ludicrous, and Anne loved it partly for these very reasons and partly because she loved Jay. Loving Jay meant loving everything she saw, particularly those things that would never have appealed to her parents.

She tried to talk to Jay above the thunder of the wind and the water but her words were tossed soundlessly away. Her eyes stang from the clouts of salty air. She was tingling cold.

It was then she saw the great horde of starlings. The sky had been empty. Suddenly it swirled with life. She pointed up towards the pinnacled domes. Were they trying to roost there? The wind was too much for them anyway. Gusts took them, rolled them, flung them back. Combined now with the sounds of the sea and the great gale could be heard the concerted squawks and yelps of the starlings. There were surely hundreds and thousands of them, a black tumult that blew, dispersed and gathered itself again above the fantastic roof of the theatre. They were like smoke, black multi-specked smoke, the individual birds so many flecks of soot. They moved in frantic unison, as one, but seemingly terrified and panicky, low above the grey green swell of the waves now, so low that watching them you felt they must drown, then up again in one flexed black swirl, fanning out above the pier and the sea only to form themselves again as a black dense liquid, poured and funnelled, controlled by some invisible wizard in the sky and its cold breath, the wind.

Breathless, Anne watched them, standing there, holding Jay's hand. It was as if a madness had gripped the starlings. She knew she would never forget this crazy multitude, and it seemed to her even then, as she stood there, silent, engrossed, that there must surely be a meaning in this image of hectic, hopeless energy. The starlings had made a terrible mistake in choosing this unlikely and unsuitable place to roost, but it was a mistake they would not admit to. Oblivious of the danger they rallied and swerved, so that gathering together or flailing apart it was always the slippery, foolish golden domes they wanted.

Nothing else would please them. Nothing else would do.

⋆ ⋆ ⋆ ⋆

For eleven rebellious months in the late sixties Anne had lived with Jay in a shabby bedsit in one of those tall-gabled houses in Bella Vista Avenue. That area of town was demolished fifteen years later, to make way for the expressway, that road of opportunity, blessed by business people and commuters and cursed by those who saw the Welsh way of life threatened, eroded constantly by unwelcome influxes from the east.

The Welsh way of life was what Anne left behind her when she moved in with Jay. Now, looking back, she was astonished at her own courage. I couldn't do it now, she thought, but then, of course, there'd been something in the air, hadn't there? She was responding to a great upsurge of energy, a yearning for change. If it was really only an illusion of freedom, she certainly hadn't seen it as illusory at the time. She'd been quite exceptionally happy. Days would see her at work in the building society office, evenings at home with Jay, unless the band were playing somewhere. She closed her eyes and was back in their tall, cold room. She kept it neat, clean, was proud of it all, the huge white paper lampshades, the great saggy cushions on the floor, the ancient sofa completely covered with multicoloured batik cottons. One part of the room, half concealed behind a bamboo and raffia screen, was the kitchen, nothing but a sink, a draining board and a mini-cooker. There was an old deal table. No cupboards. Their pots and pans and cutlery were in boxes, as was their food. These cramped conditions didn't stop Anne from cooking imaginative meals. It was all a novelty, splendid, soaring.

'You're keeping him,' her father would say, 'and he's letting you, the skunk.'

But Anne would defend Jay immediately, insisting that he did pay his way whenever he could, incredulous that her father could so loathe the man she loved so totally.

She was eighteen. She would never feel like this about anyone again. Even now, as she thought of Jay's hands, his thin bony face, the way his hair curled into the nape of his neck, she was swamped by feeling. Oh yes, she tried to make her parents see that Jay was no ogre, that he was gentle, sensitive, talented, special. That he meant the world to her. That all their opposition would never shake her confidence in him. Sometimes he worked at lunch time behind the bar at The Crescent across the road. She told them this but it didn't go down well. Her father was strictly teetotal. That she'd attached herself to a longhaired layabout who played in a band and served in a public house, that she'd given up her 'A' levels, left home, left school to get a job to keep them both, and was now living in sin .... She'd brought shame on the family. For a few weeks her father kept trying to get Anne to change her mind, to come back home, turning up on the doorstep with the same arguments, the same blustering anger, the same pleas.

Eventually the visits stopped. There was no communication now between bohemian bedsit land and the austere village in the hills. Its straight tight-lipped terraces, its ornate chapels, its stately monkey puzzle trees and laurel bushes were only nine miles away as the crow flies. Nine miles and a different world. Anne's house was at the end of the village, serenely respectable behind its railings. This was the third generation of the firm Jerome Roberts and Son, coal merchants and haulage contractors, though this time there was no son to carry on the business. As far as the present Jerome was concerned there was now no daughter either. Anne had turned her backs on them, rejected their teaching, their guidance, their way of life. Her mother, a shallow, sentimental woman, who had captured Jerome with her big dark eyes, and her charming soprano voice at the eisteddfodau they'd attended as young people, and of which they were still bastions and staunch supporters, cried incessantly, kept trying, quite hopelessly, to prevail on Jerome, to make him understand that turning his back on his one daughter was unnatural, was insupportable. It did no good whatsoever. If she'd been a better judge of character Mair might have seen that what these two had most in common was their stubborn pride. Neither one of them would back down now. Ever.

Bella Vista Avenue had once been a good address. Some well-preserved family homes and boarding houses still persevered, but for the most part the multiple lets had lost the tall houses their dignity. They attracted a feckless, drifting population, young for the most part, picturesque misfits, who worked, if they worked at all, in seasonal jobs, in the arcades, in cheap cafés, in bars and on the fairground, or were, like Jay, somehow involved in the world of entertainment, however precariously, and with whatever doubtful degree of success.

Anne loved the atmosphere around her, so utterly different from the staid sameness of home. She was unusual in having a proper job, and was teased about it by Dougie, the hugely muscular and hairy drummer in Jay's band. Dougie's succession of blonde, stoned girlfriends studied Anne as if she'd come from a different planet. It amused her. These pretty, vapid girls had quantities of peroxide hair piled up on top and wore tight skirts and see-through blouses. Anne was fascinated by their shoes, old-fashioned strappy flimsy things with spindly heels. These were girl rockers really, stuck in a time-warp. Dougie seemed to have an endless identikit supply of them. He was all right really, though some of the other band members worried her. She knew they were on to any kind of drug they could get their hands on, and Carl in particular frightened her. He had hard, cruel eyes. He was the singer, moodily good looking, but, Anne felt, a decidedly bad influence on Jay.

Again looking back, she was suddenly struck by the fact that she did in many ways mother Jay. That wasn't surprising. He'd been brought up by his grandparents, stern, unimaginative people. He needed mothering and Anne was quite happy to provide the uncritical affection he'd never had.

Best of all for Anne were the quiet evenings she spent with Jay, just the two of them, on their own. She would sit in the corner on one of those big saggy cushions and listen to him play his guitar. He wanted to be good, really good. He practised for hours, endless complicated riffs, and Anne would enter his dream of fame and stardom, becoming part of his music, an extension of his fantasy. It was a fantasy time altogether.

In the summer they would walk the long promenade, arms entwined about each other, in and out of the canopied trees hung with lamps. Sometimes a marmalade cat would appear, crossing the road from its vantage point on a hotel verandah to join them. They started to look out for it, as if it was half theirs, loving its cheeky face and its friendliness, its strangely querulous miaow. Once it followed them a little way down the pier, but it was afraid of the gaps between the boards, the dark water below. Anne and Jay walked on together, the huge sky above them tremulous and kind, the gently swishing waves beneath their feet a soft fretful orchestration.

When winter came to their towering room they had their love to keep them warm. They'd sit together in the half-dark for hours, the street light outside their one shadowy illuminator, drinking mugs of soup and eating plates of toast. Sometimes Jay would try out a new tune. Sometimes Anne would supply the words. They'd improvise, creating for a moment a triumphant novelty of cadence and meaning. Only seldom did their joint efforts stand up to the sharper, more searching light of day.

Always their songs were love songs.

⋆ ⋆ ⋆ ⋆

It's a long time ago now, Anne thought. She stood on that same bank they'd stood on, way back on the night of the starlings. The spindly pines had gone. Instead of the rough seeded grass on the sloping bank it was all stiffly manicured lawn now, with beds of red and yellow tulips. Behind Anne traffic on the expressway whirred by. The sweep of the road that sliced through the town had long since taken Bella Vista Avenue and her sister streets into oblivion. The truncated pier was still there, just, closed to the public now because it was unsafe. The baroque domed theatre was a run-down wreck, its gold paint peeling. For Sale notices were pasted to its undulating roof—the council had decided not to waste any more money on its upkeep.

Well over twenty years had passed since she'd stood here that night with Jay, watching the starlings rise and fall, swarming like crazed bees against a gargantuan sea-lashed hive. She remembered the sound of the waves and the wind, the way her voice had been swept away from her by buffetings of storm.

When she thought of Jay she thought of the most vivid person she'd ever known. No one could compare with him, nothing could match the life they'd had together. She thought of the night she'd slept alone that last time, her unaccustomed anxiety, her fitful troubled turning. The band had a booking in Blackpool, would be playing till the early hours, would doss down on some friend's floor very probably, would be back in the morning. And back they did all come except for Jay. He'd been found dead, stretched out on someone's sofa, choked on his own vomit after a night's heavy drinking with the lads. And of the lot of them, it was generally Jay who drank the least. It was so unfair. Anne looked up at hairy, hilarious Dougie, now so quiet, at Carl, the hard man. She was suddenly convulsed by a great gush of hatred. Why was he alive when her Jay was dead?

Jerome and Mair appeared a few days later. They'd seen the report of Jay's death in the paper. Anne managed to be civil to them. Nothing more. Part of her felt that her father was gloating, that he was pleased Jay was dead. There was no way she would return home. Did they expect her to come running back to them?

As far as she was concerned nothing would ever make her leave Bella Vista Avenue.

Perhaps on the rebound, who can say, Anne was married a few months later, to Ronald. Her manager at work, he was a good deal older, and with his solidity and sobriety he would have been the ideal husband, no doubt, in her parents' eyes. He didn't speak Welsh, but apart from that he was perfect.

Anne didn't invite Jerome and Mair to the wedding. She didn't even tell them about it. Ronald had been unhappy about this, feeling he could hardly ask his own family to the wedding if Anne was adamantly not inviting hers. They got married very quietly in the end, in a registry office, in the company of just a few friends. The first thing Anne's parents knew about it was the account they read in the paper.

Within a year Robert had been promoted to manage a far larger branch in the Midlands. Again he tried to persuade Anne to make things up with her parents. She stubbornly shook her head. It was only with the birth of her first child, Thomas, that Anne relented, writing to Jerome and Mair, telling them her news. She was so glad she'd done this because only three months later Jerome was dead. Anne, to Ronald's surprise, was devastated. He was not to know that she wept for her father some of the tears she'd been unable to weep for Jay. He was not to know that on one level she quite simply wept for her life.

Over the years Mair had grown increasingly frail and confused. She finally had to leave the old family home and accept the orderly comforts of a nursing home instead. Anne and

Ronald made sure it was the very best place of its kind, a pleasant building, once a hotel, with fine views of the bay.

This had been their first visit to Mair since her move. Leaving Ronald waiting for her in the car, Anne walked for a while, reliving the past Ronald knew nothing about, all the old haunts, the echo of them. Though there'd been visits over the years to the children's grandmother's home in the village in the hills, Anne had never come back here.

Something died in me when Jay died, she told herself.

Today the face of the sea was placid. There was just the one seagull flying low and lazily over the waves.

Special

She was six and her father was very ill but she did not know this. He was in the big hospital for an operation on his spine and it was fifty/fifty chance they said, though she did not know what that meant either. Anyway, so she could be near daddy and visit him every day, her mother had come to stay with her old friend, Lally. Her husband was a vicar, a man with gingery hair and a gold filling, who smiled a lot and forgot things.

As daddy was going to be in hospital for some weeks, and would have to convalesce for a while after that, she was to go to school here, in this village that was so different from home, with its mountains and its great piles of broken slate and its mist and rain.

Here it was the end of a golden summer, and the tiny school under the horse chestnut trees was a welcoming place with a coal fire in the one big classroom. Miss Penny, the teacher, brought her dog to school every day. It was a collie and it slept under her table with its head on its paws and a small snore coming from it. She liked the school. She liked being the stranger from far away Wales. She taught them Welsh words and that made her special, the centre of attention, and she made them giggle and laugh when she told them *mochyn budr* meant dirty pig. Everyone went home that day saying '*mochyn budr, mochyn budr*' to their mothers and fathers, and their brothers and sisters too, who went to the big school in the town where daddy's hospital was.

Lally and the vicar (they called him Justin) had one boy who was seven and a half. His name was Daniel. In the beginning he had not been very friendly with her really. He had his own friends, Barty Garret and Bobby Clegg, and he liked to do things with them because they had a gang and a den of their own up in the woods behind the church. But after the day of *mochyn budr* everyone wanted to be her friend, so he was too.

Before that Barty Garret and Bobby Clegg had come twice to the vicarage and Daniel had gone off on his own with them, saying girls couldn't join their gang, and leaving her to play by herself, which she quite liked in a way because the vicarage garden was huge and rambling and had a gazebo. A gazebo was a very wonderful thing to have in your garden. This one was made of a dark curling wood. It smelt strongly of something, creosote Lally said it was, and it had the lawn mower inside, and scythes and shears and the big spades and garden forks.

Anyway, after they said she could join their gang after all, she went with them to the woods behind the church where their den was. There was a good path up there, sandy and clear through the pines on the ridge above the village, and their den was a real one with a broken desk in it and boxes to sit on. There was a swing outside on a tree nearby with a strong low branch at just the right height and a thick rope with a big knot at the end that you tucked your legs around when you were swinging.

She was beginning to learn something about herself, an important thing, that being different and coming from a far away place where they could speak another language altogether, gave her a kind of magic in the eyes of the other children. She was definitely special. They listened to what she had to say, and having such an audience made her, well, put frills on it, as her mother sometimes said. 'Megan's got such an imagination,' Lally would say, but her mother kept telling her to stick to the facts. Megan did generally, but facts could get dreary. She started to say things that weren't quite true and the children believed it all, until she told them her uncle was a wizard like Merlin in the King Arthur book Miss Penny read to them on Friday afternoons. One girl, Margaret Thwaite, had heard that her father was in hospital. If her uncle was a wizard he could make her father better, couldn't he? If he was a real proper wizard there would've been no reason for her father to go to hospital in the first place. She had to think of something quick and clever to say, so she said things would have been much worse if her uncle hadn't put a magic on her father's back. That if her uncle hadn't been able to use his spells, her father might already have died.

This worked with the others, though Margaret Thwaite still looked grumpy, and said she didn't believe any of it. The trouble was, thinking like that about her father dying, had made her feel afraid. It hadn't occurred to her before that he just might die. She started to cry, right there and then, in school, and started crying all over again when she got back to the vicarage. There her mother and Lally tried to reassure her. That night after tea she went along with her mother when Justin drove her to the hospital to see daddy. She was pleased to see that he was half sitting up in bed. He did look thinner and there was a pale look in his face, and creases that hadn't been there before, but he was nowhere near dying, Megan was sure. She realised, though, that being special the way she was at the moment, made some people, people like Margaret Thwaite, not like her. She was glad she wasn't going to be here forever, and suddenly for the first time she felt just a bit homesick for mountains, mist and rain, and great heaps of broken slate.

Soon it would be Harvest Festival. The school would be taking part in the service in the church and all the children would be collecting flowers and fruit from the people who lived in the village, and they'd also collect tinned food which could go to the old age pensioners. There was going to be a harvest supper in the church hall and there were going to be handbells.

'How would you like to be a campanologist, Megan?' Justin asked her.

It was only the children who went to Sunday School regularly that could take part in the handbells. Margaret Thwaite was one of them, which wasn't very nice. Megan made sure she was standing right on the other side of the other row, at the back, so she was nowhere near her and didn't have to look at her. Daniel was playing the handbells too, of course, but Barty Garret and Bobby Clegg weren't in it. They didn't go to Sunday School, though Justin, smiling and showing the gold filling, had told Megan that Barty had started to turn up mysteriously last year, just before the Christmas party. And after the party he'd stopped coming, just like that. Megan thought that was an awful thing to do.

Well, the Harvest Festival service came and went and the church looked beautiful. The harvest supper was even better. Everyone enjoyed the handbells and the singing and the food was wonderful and so much of it! For the first time in her life Megan tasted two lovely new things. One was oatcakes, hot and swimmy in butter, and the other was little pickled onions.

The nights were drawing in, and you could feel winter in the air now. There was even a bit of frost at night and there was talk of daddy being well enough to leave the convalescent home soon. Bonfire night was coming. Daniel, Megan, Barty Garret and Bobby Clegg, started to collect all the wood and all the odds and ends they could find for the bonfire they were going to have in the vicarage garden.

One day, it was a Saturday, Daniel had an idea. Why not go into town and buy some fireworks? There was only the post office in the village, and they didn't have fireworks there, and although Justin and Lally would be buying fireworks for their bonfire on the big night, Daniel and Megan thought it would be good to have some of their own. Daniel wanted to get some jumping jacks but Megan hated them. She hated bangers too. She intended to get some beautiful Roman candles and a Catherine wheel. Between them they had more than a pound in saved up pocket money. Daniel thought it was a good idea not to tell Justin or Lally or Megan's mother what they were doing exactly. They just said they'd be going out.

'We'll take a short cut over the fields', said Daniel.

'That doesn't mean we have to go on the Rickety Rackety, does it?' Megan asked in a worried voice.

The Rickety Rackety was a sort of bridge but not really, and it was the only way over a quite wide stream between two fields. Earlier, just a few weeks back, when it felt like summer still and there was only a trickle of water, Megan hadn't minded it, but lately it had been raining a lot, and the stream was more like a river by now. The Rickety Rackety was made of two sheets of rusty corrugated iron with a couple of bricks in the middle and what you were supposed to do was spring on to the first sheet, and then on to the bricks and somehow bounce up on to the sandy bank. Megan was not the bounciest girl, but trying to look brave in front of Daniel she did manage the leap, the balancing bit and then that last worst thing, the bounce itself. She was not looking forward to coming back though. The Rickety Rackety was glugging in a horrible way.

One of the very first shops they came to in the town sold fireworks. They spent a long time deciding which ones they'd get and afterwards the man in the shop put them all in a big brown paper bag half folded over. Even through the paper you could smell the gunpowder. Megan thought it was just about the most exciting smell she'd ever smelt. It seemed to her to be a secretive smell and full of danger. The Rickety Rackety was dangerous enough though. Sure enough, by the time they got back to the stream, the corrugated sheets were even more underwater and the whole thing was making very strange noises indeed.

'Isn't there another way we could go?' she asked.

'No,' said Daniel.

'You'd better hold the fireworks in case I can't do it,' she said, her voice trying to sound strong.

'Course you can do it', Daniel said, but very sensibly he took the fireworks from her. They'd been taking it in turns to carry the bag till then. He jumped and made it look easy, but he also made the corrugated sheets slip a bit, and by now the bricks in the middle were under water completely.

Well, Megan jumped, and it was a disaster. She landed sideways on the first sheet and it tilted somehow and tipped her up. There she was in the middle of the stream, soaked to her waist and her shoes full of gravelly stuff. She was determined not to cry but she couldn't help it. It just happened, and as she tried to scramble out she found the water by the far bank was deeper than she'd thought. Daniel tried to get to her, reaching out an arm to her after carefully putting the fireworks in his pocket. That was a stupid thing to do though, because as she grabbed his hand she pulled him in! In the end, after a lot of yelling they managed to crawl up onto the bank, but by now they were both soaked through, and yes, the fireworks were ruined. When they got back to the vicarage it was hot baths for the pair of them. Later on, when Barty Garret and Bobby Clegg came round, Daniel went off with them and said she wasn't allowed in their gang anymore.

'I don't care,' she said, but of course she cared very much really.

Suddenly she just didn't want to live here any longer. She wanted to go home, to go back to her own school. She didn't cry though. She knew it was a matter of waiting, of being patient. It was not easy to be patient but sooner or later she really would be saying goodbye to everyone here and life would go back to being like it was before daddy had to go to hospital.

Megan went and sat by herself in the study where Justin wrote his sermons. The study was a cold room but Megan liked it because of the the wooden panels on the walls and the deep heavy chairs with great wings to them. She sat in one of these chairs in the window, looking out at the big copper beech tree. She swallowed hard and told herself to be brave and sensible. Justin was out there on the lawn raking gold leaves and lemon leaves and putting them all in a huge damp sack. She waved at him. When he beckoned to her to come out into the garden she shook her head. Already she felt she was slipping away from being here. In her imagination she wasn't here at all. What really mattered was home, home where she belonged. Nothing that happened here was important anymore.

Within two days the news was that her father was coming along nicely. He'd seen the specialist again (Megan was very proud of the fact that her father had seen the specialist) and he'd said that as long as he took things very easy for a month or two yet, he could go home.

Megan was so glad to be back she felt she would burst out of her skin. She was thrilled just to sleep in her own bedroom and in her own bed. Far away now was the spite of Margaret Thwaite and the moodiness of Daniel. Far away was the need to put on an act all the time, to weave in and out of all the tales she'd told, so that in the end she couldn't remember what she'd said and what she hadn't. Here she didn't have to be special anymore. She was simply herself and she felt she could breathe again.

On her first morning back home she woke up early and straight away, when she saw where she was, the different light through the curtains, she ran to the window. It looked out over the steep valley side, down to the slag heaps and the chapel with its patterned slate roof, navy with a sort of grey and violet zigzag. The spindly silver birches that grew on the lip of the waste slate were glistening in the thin light and the watery air.

Acknowledgements

Acknowledgements are due to *Planet*, where 'Glut' first appeared. 'Women of a Certain Age' first appeared in *New Welsh Review*, and 'The Man from Kurdistan' in *Drawing Down The Moon* (Seren, 1995).

About the Author

Glenda Beagan lives in Rhuddlan, Denbighshire. She was educated at the University of Wales, Aberystwyth and at the University of Lancaster. Her previous collection of short stories, *The Medlar Tree*, appeared from Seren in 1992. She has also published a collection of poetry, *Vixen* (Honno, 1996).

The Medlar Tree

The Medlar Tree introduces a host of ordinary and extraordinary characters: Gypsy Hayes, who really *can* read the future but doesn't like what she sees; slightly sinister old Mrs Mossop (the saddist); the terribly embarrassed young Hafwen; Mrs Jenkins, Sgubor Fawr, who every so often screams for a day. A French teacher waiting for her environmentally-sound lover, the mysterious and escaping Mrs Prosser, the poppy growing Laura, are characters on the brink of revelations which will transform their lives and surprise the reader.

"... here is a truly gifted writer at work" — John Emyr, *Barn*

"... an uncanny ability to render a character primarily through descriptions of objects or landscape" — *Belles Lettres*